PRAISE FOR JAMES MARSHALL'S
NINJA VERSUS PIRATE FEATURING ZOMBIES

"Chaotic, crazy, and undeniably captivating, *NVPFZ* is the quirkiest take yet on the zombie genre. First in a series that is sure to be a smash with the gaming generation."

—*Library Journal*

". . . if you're anything like me, you will laugh hysterically and feel vaguely guilty over it and wonder if maybe there's something wrong with you."

—**Carrie Harris,**
author of *Bad Taste in Boys*

"Readers who like their literary escapism on the psychotropic side should definitely seek out and read this stroboscopic debut. Bomb disposal suit not included—but highly recommended."

—**Barnes & Noble**

". . . a good old-fashioned spin-your-head-around-twice mindfu@#."

—**Corey Redekop,**
Husk

JAMES MARSHALL

ZOMBIE VERSUS FAIRY FEATURING ALBINOS

ChiZine Publications

FIRST EDITION

Zombie Versus Fairy Featuring Albinos © 2013 by James Marshall
Cover artwork © 2013 by Erik Mohr
Cover design © 2013 by Samantha Beiko
Interior design © 2013 by Danny Evarts

Distributed in Canada by
HarperCollins Canada Ltd.
1995 Markham Road
Scarborough, ON M1B 5M8
Toll Free: 1-800-387-0117
e-mail: hcorder@harpercollins.com

Distributed in the U.S. by
Diamond Book Distributors
1966 Greenspring Drive
Timonium, MD 21093
Phone: 1-410-560-7100 x826
e-mail: books@diamondbookdistributors.com

Library and Archives Canada Cataloguing in Publication

Marshall, James, 1973-
    Zombie versus fairy featuring albinos / James Marshall.

(How to end human suffering ; 2)
Also issued in electronic format.
ISBN 978-1-77148-141-0

    I. Title. II. Series: Marshall, James, 1973- How to end human suffering ; 2.

PS8626.A78Z64 2013   C813'.6   C2013-900787-3

CHIZINE PUBLICATIONS
Toronto, Canada
www.chizinepub.com
info@chizinepub.com

Edited and copyedited by Samantha Beiko
Proofread by Kelsi Morris and Zara Ramaniah

 Canada Council   Conseil des arts
for the Arts   du Canada

We acknowledge the support of the Canada Council for the Arts which last year invested $20.1 million in writing and publishing throughout Canada.

ONTARIO ARTS COUNCIL
CONSEIL DES ARTS DE L'ONTARIO
50 YEARS OF ONTARIO GOVERNMENT SUPPORT OF THE ARTS
50 ANS DE SOUTIEN DU GOUVERNEMENT DE L'ONTARIO AUX ARTS

Published with the generous assistance of the Ontario Arts Council.

Printed in Canada

ZOMBIE VERSUS FAIRY FEATURING ALBINOS

CHAPTER ONE

A Depressed Zombie In The Anti-Depression–Era Depression

I yell at my wife, Chi, asking her if she washed my pants, and she hollers back, "No, of course not," and I yell, "They look clean," and a few seconds later, she staggers into the bedroom carrying a human foot.

She grinds it—the ragged skin, chewed meat, dried blood part—onto my thigh. "Better?" she asks, staring at the new stain on my trousers.

I look down at it, disgusted. "Yeah." I hate this. All of this. I despise it. I loathe my life. I detest everyone and everything in it. It's torture to me: the routine, the monotony, the drudgery.

A couple of nights ago, I heard Chi talking to one of her friends. "I always wanted a man who could cry," she said. "Just not all the time."

Now, staring at the blood-stain she just smeared onto my trousers, not hiding the irritation in her voice, she says, "Why couldn't you do that yourself, Buck?"

I undo the top two buttons of my shirt. "I'm helpless." I jerk my tie to the side.

"I don't know what you'd do," she agrees, "if I wasn't around."

The other night, while eavesdropping on Chi, I overheard her say, conspiratorially, "His emotions aren't the only part of him to go soft, if you know what I'm saying."

Constance, the cat, slinks into the bedroom. Constance mocks me constantly. She's so at ease. So self-assured. She's so comfortable in her own skin. I hate her. The fire of life burns under her ash-grey coat.

Chi throws the human foot against the wall as hard as she can. When it hits the floor, Constance hurries over to it and starts nibbling. As Constance eats, Chi lurches around our bedroom, messing things up. She pulls apart a pillow's stuffing, scattering it on the unmade bed. She jerks out the only drawer left in the dresser, dropping it on the floor. The drawer is empty, like the gesture. Chi performs these actions without thinking. She does them because she's supposed to. Like somebody is watching. "What time is your appointment again?"

"Three." I tuck in my shirt. Then I yank out half of it.

"You tell him you took a shower."

"I will."

"And you used soap."

"I'll tell him."

"I can still smell you." When she turns on me, I can tell by her expressionless face and emotionless eyes she's revolted.

Constance stops nibbling on the human foot and looks at me, judgmentally. She finds me wanting. Lacking.

"I'll roll around in some garbage before I get to work."

"You'd better."

Our non-living room is covered in blood: the hardwood floor is streaked with it; the walls are splattered with it; there's a lot on the ceiling. When you walk into the non-living room, you think, "Something terrible happened here." And it did. And it keeps happening. The smell is atrocious. It's feces mixed with sick. You can't breathe. You gag. Flies aren't individual insects here. They're cells. They form a loose body. A monster. A cloud that swarms. It's a panic attack. It eats and waits. For what? More to eat and its babies? Is there any difference?

When she finished decorating it, Chi looked at me, satisfied, and said, "What do you think?"

I didn't say, "I'm a zombie." I didn't say, "I don't think." Instead, I said, "It's good, Chi."

Before I leave for work, I watch my wife. She stumbles around on broken grey high heels, making sure Francis Bacon is ready for school and getting herself ready for work. She looks for her purse between the partially-consumed human corpses sprawled on the floor, wearing grotesque masks of death. Her grey legwarmers, stiff with the stuff of life and its absence, are scrunched down over her calves. She searches for her keys. Her disgusting legwarmers partially cover teeth-torn skinny black pants. What did she do with Francis Bacon's lunch? A fingernail-shredded, knee-length, formerly-shiny silver dress hides the more lurid teeth marks in her pants. She can't find the quarterly report. A blood-smeared, white, dress shirt collar sticks up from under a bullet-holey and knife-slashed brown cashmere sweater she's wearing under an open knee-length black jacket. How does she misplace everything? Where does everything go?

"Look under the torso, Chi."

Groan

"I don't know why I don't help you. I really don't."

Time passes. That's what we tell ourselves. One minute, we're here. The next minute, we're somewhere else but we're still here. What's changed? Anything?

On my way to work, at an intersection, I watch a wild dog lope across a street perpendicular to the one I'm on. The dog's tongue hangs out the side of its open mouth. It sees me but doesn't change its pace. With its tail between its legs, it just keeps going. I'm part of the scenery.

I'm at the office now, sitting in a cubicle, staring at a monitor, wishing I was alive.

"Hey, Buck," says Barry, stopping by.

"Hey, Barry."

Barry Graves is a good-looking zombie and he knows it. He's been shot in the face. Twice. It's hard to tell because he's been very well-burned. And a group of kids took shovels to his head, trying to bash out his brains—but they missed, and all they did was make him better looking. Now he's so disfigured you can't even make him out. His head is one big lump of rotten, burnt, dented meat. "Did you hear about Maturity Section?" he asks, leaning against my cubicle's divider, casually.

"No."

"Some kind of riot."

"Really." I'm not interested. On my way to work, I tried to think of anything I'm interested in. I couldn't do it.

"Heads are rolling," says Barry.

"Uh huh."

"Hey, Buck?"

"Yeah?"

"Why is your cubicle so neat?"

That gets my attention. I keep forgetting to do things. Normal everyday things. The paper on my desk is stacked tidily. My computer is upright, turned on, and functioning. The receiver is hung up on my telephone. There are no fires. I didn't even notice. That's how out of it I am.

"I don't know," I confess. Awkwardly, I stand. I pick up the computer, hold it over my head, and crash it down onto the floor. I sweep all the paper off my desk.

"Anyway, I'll see you later, Buck."

"See you later, Barry."

I try to throw a stapler through a window. It just bounces off. I look at the window: the transparency of it; the apparent fragility and the surprising strength. I pick up the stapler and try again. Same result. I do it over and over, again and again, until it's lunchtime.

Then, in the cafeteria, I have a salad. Just a salad. Everybody looks at me. I don't care. After lunch, I do the stapler thing some more. At three o'clock, I go to my appointment.

I don't know how I got here. One minute I'm at work, the next minute I'm at the doctor's office. Am I forgetting things or ignoring them?

For a while, I'm in the waiting room with the others. Then I'm in the doctor's office all by myself. I can't really tell the difference.

"What can I do for you?" asks the doctor, ambling in with my file.

"I don't think there's anything you can do for me," I answer, honestly.

He tosses my file on his desk. "Okay then." He falls onto a chair. "What brings you by?"

"My wife. She made the appointment."

The doctor's white lab coat is torn, pulled halfway off his left shoulder, and stained dark red with blood. Bits of flesh are stuck to it, here and there. "She's worried about you, is she?" He turns away, opens my file, and pulls out a page. He turns back to me, holds up the piece of paper, and begins, methodically, shredding it into narrow strips.

"I guess."

I look around the office: degrees have been yanked off walls; there's shattered glass on the floor; broken picture frames have been thrown around, mindlessly, and jigsaw pieces of family photos have been strewn about, religiously. There are tongue depressors all over the place. Is that what they do here? Do they just depress our tongues? The sanitary paper that once covered the examination bed has been completely unrolled.

"Why is your wife worried about you?" asks the doctor, looking at me, interested, disinterestedly ripping what's left of a page from my file into two last shreds that fall when he lets them go.

"I'm not eating. Not sleeping. Sometimes I cry and I don't know why."

The doctor stuffs his hand into his coat pocket and fumbles out a prescription pad. He snatches a pen off his desk, scribbles something down, tears off the piece of paper, crumples it, and throws it away without looking. It hits the door and falls to the floor. "Anything else?"

"I took a shower last night. With soap."

The doctor frowns at me. His forehead doesn't change. Neither do his eyes. He frowns at me with his mind. "Why?"

"I wanted to feel clean again."

"Did you?"

"No. I still felt dead."

The doctor nods. "Yeah. It's okay." He stands, uncoordinatedly, ambles a few steps, bends at the waist, and picks up the piece of paper he crumpled and threw at the door. "We see this sometimes." He straightens up and stumbles back. When he gets to his desk, he kicks the lowest metal drawer as hard as he can several times. Then he falls onto his chair. "It's not common but it happens."

"What is it?" I'm not worried. I don't care what he says. He could say, "Buck, you're dying,'" and I wouldn't care. It'd be exactly what I want but it wouldn't make me happy. Where I am, in my head, there's no such thing as happy. It doesn't exist.

"You're depressed," says the doctor.

"I can't be depressed."

"You're married, right?"

"Right."

"Then you can be depressed."

I stare at him, vacantly.

Vacantly, he stares back. Then he says, "That was a joke."

"Good one."

"Tell me about your sex life."

"Is that another joke?"

"No."

In my mind, I picture the last time I had sex with my wife: she wears a French maid uniform. She holds a feather duster. She waves it around in the air, half-heartedly, cleaning nothing. She won't take it all the way. Later, she complains about how it makes her feel. She vows she'll never do it again. It's not open for debate.

Cleaning fetishes are among the most taboo in our community. The pornography is black-market. Underground. It's as tame as pretty living girls in short skirts bending at the waist to pick things off the floor.

Tidying up. Cute living girls in bright yellow plastic gloves washing dishes. But, from what I hear, from what I'm told, it can get pretty racy.

Before my wife told me she'd never do it again, there's the memory of her disgusting skin where it's exposed, beyond the uniform I ask her, no, I *beg* her to leave on. It's so new, so clean. I keep my hands on it and my eyes on it and I try to concentrate on it. I try not to think of the truth: my wife's open wounds and festering sores and her expressionless face as I lay on my back while she uses my rigidity, my inflexibility, my thoughtless conformity to biological processes I don't understand and probably wouldn't approve of even if I did, for her . . . whatever it is, amusement, or her own mindless acceptance of physiological impulses she doesn't comprehend.

I wonder. Is this love?

"It's not like it used to be," I admit.

"Pretty sure you're depressed," says the doctor, opening and flattening the paper he crumpled a few moments ago. "I wrote you a prescription."

"Okay."

He crumples it back up and throws it at my face. Conveniently, it bounces onto my lap. The doctor stabs the pen into his stomach, repeatedly, until it punctures and stays there. Satisfied it will remain, the doctor, unsteadily, lifts his head. "Yeah, so get that filled, follow the directions, and you should be as good as dead. Eat some human flesh and don't bathe or clean your clothes. You have to look after yourself, Buck."

"Is there anything I should look out for while taking this medication?"

"The most common side effects are insomnia, loss of appetite, and sexual dysfunction."

"So I could feel better and never know it because the side effects of this medication are exactly the same as the problems I already have."

"Hypothetically. Why?"

"No reason."

"Hey, you work in Reproduction Section, don't you?"

"Yeah."

"Are you going to make your quota?"

"Easily."

"Good."

Precariously, I get up. For a minute, I just stand there, wondering what I'd do right now if I weren't depressed. Then I pick up my chair and hurl it at a filing cabinet.

"That's it, Buck," says the doctor. "That's the spirit."

When I weave my way out of the doctor's office, I walk unevenly past all the other zombies, sitting there dumbly, staring emptily, dripping drool from the corners of their mouths. One has a machete embedded in his side, spilling white sausage from the wound. Another holds her own severed leg, dangling purple ground meat from her stump. The others reach their stiff arms out for something: death maybe, for death to return; that briefest of moments when we died, when we passed from living, actually being alive, really alive, truly alive, to just being undead. In disorganized chairs, nonaligned chairs, in chairs purposefully arranged haphazardly, in the waiting room, all the zombies sit with nearly straight bodies.

I walk outside and keep going. I walk and walk. After an hour or so, I end up on a dead-end street. There's a chain-link fence keeping me from going any farther. Beyond the fence and through it, I see a group of living teenagers hanging out behind a strip-mall where all the deliveries are made to the backs of stores. The teenagers are gathered among big dumpsters where the day's waste is brought out, taken away, and turned into energy to make more waste.

The teenagers are skateboarding. They're practicing tricks on the pavement. They're making use of the curbs, the railings, and all the other unnatural obstacles: jumping them, sliding down them, riding up, turning around, and gliding back down them. I stick my fingers into the metal diamonds and stare at the teenagers—at the life in them—through the chain-link fence. I think about their DNA. The teenagers are made of chains but they still think they're free. Free from what? Their looks? Their brains? Their environment? The strange age into which they were born? Free to do what? Become a zombie? It's so sad. Is there anything sadder than a slave who believes he or she is free? I don't know. Until they get blurry in my eyes from the tears that don't come from staring and wouldn't come at all if I were normal, I watch the teenagers.

Finally, I pull my fingers free from the double helixes in the chain-link fence and stumble away. After staggering around for a while, I find a drugstore. I pull open the door and amble carefully through the orderly aisles. I try not to knock anything off the organized shelves. It's atypical zombie behaviour but I can't bring myself to wreck anything. I like the clean. I like the bright and inviting products standing in rows. I like the smell of the perfume in the makeup section. In the back of the drugstore, I find a fairy.

Some humans think medicine is science but it's not. It's part art but it's mostly magic. Pills, for example, are a hundred percent fairy dust.

The pharmacist fairy is a short, slender, green-haired girl. Her tiny wings stick through slits in the back of her uniform, fluttering nervously. She's gorgeous. All fairies are gorgeous but this one is especially gorgeous. It makes me feel worse. It reminds of what I am now, what I was then, and what I can never be again. I know I wouldn't be able to see her for what she really is if I were still alive but it doesn't make me feel any better. I stare at her wings. They're delicate; transparent. Black lines segment them, like veins in leaves. It's hard to imagine those flimsy things lifting her off the ground, even though she's so slight. There's a rectangular white badge pinned to her white uniform. There are black letters on the badge: Fairy_26.

Disgusted by myself on her behalf, acutely aware of my grossness, and self-conscious of my gnarled, senseless, grey-green hand, I push the crumpled prescription across the counter to her.

"You want me to fill this?" she stammers. Her supple hand darts out, grabs the prescription, and jerks it away.

I grunt and nod.

"Okay, you want me to fill your prescription," she says, nodding rapidly, trying to be brave. "It'll take a while. You can have a seat over there." She points in a fluid but quick way at a couple of chairs arranged side-by-side at the end of a nearby aisle. She drops her hand so she's holding both arms tight against her sides. "If you want, I mean."

I groan. I stagger away. I fall into a smooth plastic chair.

Nowadays, zombies work in conjunction with supernatural creatures, like the fairies, with whom they've struck an uneasy alliance. The war between zombies and supernatural creatures occurred several thousand years ago. It's still a sore point with supernatural creatures, though, all of whom love human beings and hate what zombies do to them. In fact, it's rumoured there are factions of supernatural creature revolutionary groups intent on overthrowing zombies but I don't know anything about that.

An elf saunters in as I wait for my prescription to be filled with fairy dust. The elf is dressed in a skinny black suit with an extremely tall black top hat. Without seeing me, he goes to the pharmacy counter and puts his arms on it, stretching out the back of his jacket and making it shiny. "Hey, Fairy_26," he calls.

"Get lost," she whispers. She's standing partially obscured by shelves of different sized pill bottles. I can see half of her. Her head is down and she's pouring my pink happiness onto a blue tray where she can measure it out in daily doses.

"Come on, Fair. I want to talk to you."

She pauses. When she speaks again, it's like she's forgotten I'm here. "Well, I don't want to talk to you. And besides, we don't have anything to talk about."

"I think we do."

"It's over," she says. "Get it through your head."

"Fairy_26." He says her name like he's saying, "I know you don't mean that." Then he says, "Come here. Please."

Fairy_26 walks up to the counter. She glances over at me.

"Come closer, Fair. Jeez. I'm not going to bite you."

Fairy_26 looks down, shyly, and leans closer.

The elf reaches across the counter with both hands, grabs Fairy_26 by the back of the head and pulls her to him, trying to kiss her. Both hands on his chest, Fairy_26 struggles to get away. I moan, get up, and stumble toward the elf.

He sees me, lets go of Fairy_26, and staggers away. He backs into a display. He tumbles to the ground like the bottles he knocks down and scatters across the floor. His tall black top hat falls off. Staring at me, wide-eyed, he scrambles, gets back on his feet, grabs his hat (half-crushing it in the process) and runs out of the pharmacy.

After he leaves, I make my rigid-legged and arms-outstretched way back to my chair and tumble into its smooth curved plastic.

"I'm sorry about that," says Fairy_26.

I groan in a way that conveys it wasn't a problem.

Even though it's perfect, she tries to fix her bright green hair with her fingers. I stare at her warm pink-orange hands: the ease with which they bend and flex. I look at her fingernails, how flawless they are: unbroken from clawing, fighting, and killing; tearing flesh from people, eating it, loving it.

"He's such a jerk," she says, going back to work. "I don't know why it took me so long to figure it out."

I moan, sympathetically.

"He cheated on me and he can't figure out why I won't take him back," she scoffs. "I deserve better than that. I think more highly of myself than that, you know? I'm not some brain-dead bimbo with zero self-esteem."

I nod, encouragingly.

"Listen to me ramble on," she says. "What do you care? You have problems of your own."

She goes back to counting pills.

When she stops talking, something happens to me. Something physical. I feel it: a sense of loss. It takes me a minute to figure out what it is: her voice. I miss her voice. Like being alive. I took it for granted when it was happening. When it disappeared, I realized how significant it was. Not necessarily good or right or true. Just significant.

Clumsily, I get up and go to the counter. Turned away and busy, Fairy_26 fails to notice. I bang my stiff hand down onto the shiny silver bell. It scoots across the counter and falls on the floor on the other side of the counter. I curse myself for my awkwardness but at least the noise gets her attention.

"Do you need something?" she asks, not afraid anymore or, at least, less afraid now.

I put my hand to my mouth and wave my fingers there.

"Oh my God," she says, horrified. "You're hungry?"

I shake my head emphatically. I point at her; at her mouth. I point to myself; my ears. I gesture from her mouth to my ears, from her mouth to my ears.

She frowns. "You want me to talk some more?"

I nod and nod.

"That makes you the first person I've ever met who wants me to talk some more," she says, turning away, going back to work with the pills. "Most people say I never shut up. I go on and on. Normally I do it when I'm nervous but I'm nervous all the time so I go on and on all the time. That's just the way I am. I don't think it's that bad but it sure annoys some people. You wouldn't believe how upset they get when there isn't enough silence. I don't know what it is about the quiet they like. Maybe it's calm like that in their minds. My mind isn't like that. Sometimes I wish it was. Sometimes I'm glad it isn't. I think it'd get boring. I'm sorry. I know it's none of my business and I'm not supposed to do this but can I ask you why you're getting this medication? Are you really depressed?" She looks at me, over her shoulder.

On the other side of the counter, I shrug.

"I thought only humans got depressed. Living humans, I mean."

I bang my twisted hand into my chest like, "Me, too."

"What's the matter? Don't you like being a zombie?"

I shake my head.

"Huh," she says. She turns back to her tallying. "I always thought zombies liked being zombies. Don't feel bad. I mean, of course you feel bad if you're depressed, but if it makes you feel any better, and it probably won't now that I think about it, but not all human beings like the way they are either. And supernatural creatures are no different. Mostly I like the way I am but I get pretty sad too sometimes. Sometimes I just cry and cry. I'm one of those girls. I wouldn't say I'm depressed or anything but I'm definitely a crier. I bawl my eyes out constantly. It doesn't take much to get me going either. Do you wish you were a human being?" She glances at me. "An alive human being?"

I nod and nod.

"Why?"

I lift my chin at my arms stuck out in front of me. I walk around in a circle with my unbending legs.

"The stiffness?"

I nod. Then I walk toward her, mock menacingly.

She freezes.

I stop and open my crooked hands as much as I can like, "don't worry."

"You don't like being scary, either, huh?"

I shake my head.

"Sounds like you're pretty down, all right." After she fills the bottle with the right number of pills, she stuffs it in a bag, prints up the instructions and price tag, staples it to the bag, and puts the whole thing on the counter.

I give her money. She gives me change.

"I hope it helps," she says.

I turn to go.

"Wait. Hold on." She grabs her purse. "I think I'm going to take the rest of the day off because of the stress of you."

My shoulders fall.

"No, that's just my excuse," she assures me. "I was scared at first but I didn't know you then. I'm not scared of you anymore." She rethinks. "Is that dumb? You're not going to eat my brain or try to turn me into a zombie or anything, are you?

I shake my head.

"Okay," she says. "I'm not scared of you anymore. You want to go somewhere and hang out? I don't have any zombie friends. Do you have any fairy friends?"

I shake my head.

"Do you want a fairy friend?"

I shrug.

"Not overly enthusiastic but I'll take it." She smiles. She puts her hand on my outstretched arm. She looks at the point where we meet, where we touch, and then she looks up at me, happily. "Shall we?"

We walk out of the store. As soon as we turn to go down the sidewalk, I get shot in the back with an arrow.

Shocked, outraged, infuriated, Fairy_26 spins around, searching for the source. I turn, too. Fairy_26 spots him behind us, standing in front of a sporting goods store, holding a lowered bow. It's a centaur. He has the upper half of a man and the body of a horse. His upper half, the man half, is shirtless and muscular. His lower half, the horse half, is palomino: golden-tan. "Centaur111," yells Fairy_26. "What are you doing? You can't go around shooting people with arrows!"

"He's a zombie," says Centaur111, calmly.

"So what?"

"It's okay to shoot zombies with arrows."

"Who told you that?"

"Nobody had to tell me that. It's common knowledge."

I look down at the tip of the arrow. It's poking out of my chest. It doesn't hurt. Zombies don't feel much of anything, especially not physically. I yank the stick straight through my chest and drop it on the ground.

"Well, you can't go around shooting people with arrows," insists Fairy_26.

"You can if they're zombies," assures Centaur111.

"Zombies used to be human beings!"

"But they're not anymore. That's kind of my point."

"So what if they aren't anymore? So what?"

"Zombies eat people," says Centaur111. "For food," he clarifies.

"They have to. Otherwise they'll starve to death and die."

"You mean they'll die again. Zombies are already dead."

"They're undead."

"It's okay to shoot dead people with arrows. Okay, not all dead people," he admits. "But if they get up and walk around after they die, then it's okay to shoot them with arrows. Definitely."

"You can't shoot the undead with arrows!"

"Sure you can. Ask anybody. You can even shoot them with a rifle. Here. I'll show you." He trots off into the sporting goods store to get a rifle.

"We'd better get out of here," says Fairy_26, getting in front of me, taking both my hands in hers. "You're safe with me." She says it in that reassuring voice your parents used when they told you everything was going to be okay and you believed them. Then she lifts me into the sky. In the sudden rush of wind, acceleration, and surprise, I feel so good I could die. Even though I can't. Even though I'm not. I feel alive.

CHAPTER TWO

If My Wife Wasn't Already Dead, I'd Probably Kill Her

I, Buck Burger, depressed zombie, unhappy husband and failed father, hereby resolve and vow to never harm Fairy_26. In addition, I swear to protect her from those who would and could do her harm, specifically in the form of turning her from what she is now, an incredibly beautiful, kind, and carefree winged sprite, into an entirely earthbound, plodding, inflexibly self-interested zombie such as I, unfortunately, and eternally, am. Right now, Fairy_26 is holding my undead claw of a hand and pulling me—looking ahead and then back at me—happily, through the hall, leading to her apartment in a branch of a tree in downtown Fairyland.

I don't know how we got to Fairyland. It was a blur. I was so excited. We were moving so fast. Knowing how to get to Fairyland would be invaluable to zombies.

Zombies would mount an attack, hoping to massacre all the supernatural creatures, even though we'd never be able to. Supernatural creatures outmatch us in every way except one: they're compassionate. Compassion is a terrible weakness. It's what we, the zombies, exploit to survive.

Supernatural creatures love living people. They play tricks on them sometimes but they love them. I understand why they love them now. I didn't before I became depressed, but now that I do, I never want to forget.

Love of living people is what led to the tentative truce between zombies and supernatural creatures. The tentative truce continues to this day, in the form of an uneasy alliance. We, the zombies, only infect living people who, unmistakeably, embrace the zombie life. In exchange, supernatural creatures hide zombies— until it's too late—from, it should be said, most living people, as well as most signs of zombie behaviour, including but not limited to, concert hall massacres, shopping mall massacres, airport massacres—all your conventional massacres—along with general destructive behaviour on both the small personal scale and the large institutional scale. I say supernatural creatures hide zombies and signs of zombie behaviour from most living people because there's a small percentage of living people who learn or recognize the horrible truth and can, thereafter, see us for what we, unfortunately, are. These living people are few and far between and, I'm afraid, very afraid.

Reportedly, there was a time when the vast majority of the living embraced the supernatural creature life over the zombie life. That time, it seems, has passed. These days, almost all our young become zombies.

Some blame the education system; others organized religion. A few don't see the difference.

In any event, now supernatural creatures do the hard work of cleaning up after zombie rampages: they fix what we break, pick up what knock down, and organize what we disorder. They usually get most of the blood. They keep us from completely destroying ourselves. We, the zombies, tell ourselves, telepathically, supernatural creatures do it because we're so much more powerful than they are and we control them. But we know, down deep inside, that they only do it because they love people: non-undead people. They want to hide the horror from them. They hate us: zombies. Or so I mindlessly thought.

Once we're both inside Fairy_26's apartment, she closes the door, locks it, and leans back against it, smiling at me. "We made it," she says. Her hands are flat against the door.

I groan in agreement.

"Why don't you wait for me in the living room? I'm going to take a quick shower." Still beaming at me, she unbuttons her drugstore uniform top. She takes it off right in front of me. I stare at her small, perky, warm, and alive breasts. When she turns and hangs the garment up in the open closet next to the front door, I stare at her little wings and where they emerge from her wound-free back. They sprout lightly from between her shoulder blades, which jut out in a strong and angular way in comparison.

I turn away, uncomfortable. Somehow her wings and where they meet her skin are more intimate than her breasts. I stumble toward the living room.

"Turn on some music if you want," she calls after me.

I don't know if this world is bigger than mine, if we shrank, or if it's a bit of both. The carpet is spongy green moss. The walls are flowers: two walls are covered with white daisies; one wall is covered with red daisies. Every other exposed surface is warm brown wood; it has a fresh cut smell but I know it hasn't been cut; it's still alive. Like Fairy_26.

If I turn back right now, I know I'll see her take off the rest of her clothes. It's cruel. Is she doing this intentionally? To hurt me? To rub what she has—life, warmth, ease, and flexibility—in my face? Or is she just so completely unaware of what it means to me?

Whether she knows it or not, there's a stark element of viciousness to this: her beauty and how liberal she is with it. On the other hand, if she were conservative and shy, she'd probably just inflame, frustrate, and maybe even infuriate me. There's no winning with her. And me. I've never spent much time thinking about how beautiful supernatural creatures should act. It must be impossible. If you come right out and say, "Look I just want to be your friend," you seem egotistical and presumptuous but if you don't lay out the ground-rules, you might wind up leading someone on. Maybe beautiful supernatural creatures don't have it as easy as I assumed.

I don't turn on any music. I just fall onto her sofa and wait for her. The sofa is dark brown wood that flows out from the walls so fluidly it seems more like a thing of water. Its cushions are thick. They're the same spongy green moss that covers the floor. The light is bright. It pours in through an apartment-wide, floor-to-ceiling window. The whole apartment is cut off on one side. It's not a cross-sectional cut. It's right at the edge. The wall that looks like it should be there isn't but the apartment is so comfortable it doesn't feel like anything is missing. The apartment just ends and the sky begins. The sunlight flooding into the side of the tree, into the side of me, into the room where I am, sitting on soft moss that smells of freshness and life, everything I'm not, while waiting for a fairy to shower, is like nothing I've ever experienced. It's not the perfection of its brightness: it's neither glaring nor dim. It's not the perfection of its temperature: it's neither too warm nor too cool. It's the perfection of it. It's impossible. Yet I see it and feel it and know it can't be but I don't care. Can light be happy? I think this light is happy. It's not burning unimaginably in the cold dark of space and sometimes reaching out, with a flare, for something it can never touch.

I feel worse than I did before. Even though I want to be here and, if the word makes any sense coming from me, I think I'm "glad" to be here, because someone who's so everything-I-want-to-be has seen me and reacted with something other than unmistakable visceral revulsion . . . but how can a starving man, left alone with a feast, not want a bite?

I can hear the water running in the shower. She's singing a song I don't know. I'm trying to not to think of her warm smooth body moving under a spray of clear-but-strangely-white water. I'm trying not to think of her doing what I tried to do yesterday when I took a shower: getting clean. I'm trying not to imagine this:

I get up. I stagger, slowly, toward the bathroom door. With my deformed-by-death hand, I try the smooth wooden doorknob. I do it as quietly as I can. It's unlocked. I open the door. Steam enshrouds me, ghosting out into the cool behind me. I see her through the shower curtain of hanging and dripping weeping willow branches but she doesn't see me. She's lit by the bright sky pouring through the skylight. I look at her slender naked body. If I had a normal heart, it'd beat faster, harder. If I had regular blood, it'd course. It'd surge. If I could breathe like a human being, I couldn't breathe. I stumble toward the dangling willow branches. I yank them to the side. She screams. What good does screaming do? She slips, falls, gets up, backs up, away from me, slapping at my arms, which are always reaching out and which now reach out for her. The water hits me but I can't feel it. I can't feel anything but my cold hunger-lust. She's shaking her head from side to side crazily, screaming and screaming. I grab her and yank her close to me. With my mouth wide-open and my jagged broken teeth shining, I bite and tear a chunk of flesh from her neck. Blood spurts from her in a rhythmically pulsing geyser of red juice. The scream changes. It becomes a thing of pain and knowing, rather than of fear and wonder. I try to drag her from the shower but I lose my grip on her and she falls. On the mossy floor, she kicks her legs insanely. She tries in vain to staunch the colour squirting from her neck. In the shower water pooling on the green moss, her blood tries to fashion a pink outfit to cover her nakedness but it fails and swirls, reluctantly, down the tree drain. I consume her. I eat all the lovely healthy youthful parts of her. I do it so I can remain. So I can stay. Undead. I won't make her like me. She won't become a zombie. There won't be enough of her left when I'm done. It's a mercy to repay her kindness. Besides, I'm so hungry. I don't take pleasure in devouring her. I need to do it; I must. I don't do it because I want to do it; I hate it. I'm forced, through a biological imperative, to do all this, to sustain my miserable life, to prolong the monotony: the toil, the routine, the hassle. The strain. I do it because this is what everyone expects from me. I do it because this is what I have to do to be considered normal. My wife says, "Everyone has to do things they don't want to do, Buck."

And that's exactly why I *don't* do it. Because I have to. I need to. But I refuse. I won't be my hunger. I won't do what zombies say I should do. I'm still sitting on the couch. Fairy_26 is still, safely, in the shower. While I wait for her to finish, I make a telepathic call to my wife. She's probably worried.

"Buck? Where are you? You're late. You said you'd take me to get groceries, remember? What'd the doctor say?"

I never know where to start with my wife. That's part of the problem. We're always in the middle of something. Nothing ever starts or stops. It's always the middle.

"The doctor said I'm depressed, Chi."

"Depressed? What do you have to be depressed about? You have everything anyone could possibly want. You have a great job; you have a great house; you have a wife who loves you . . . wait. Is that it? Are you depressed because of me? Should we go to counselling? Barry and Deepah are going to counselling. Deepah says it's done wonders for them. She says they're like teenagers again. Are you coming home now? You said you'd take me to get groceries, remember?"

"I remember. I'll take you to get groceries. I'm just going to be a little late."

"Why? What's wrong? What's going on, Buck? Are you okay?"

"No I'm not okay, Chi. I'm depressed."

"About what?"

"I don't know. I just found out I'm depressed."

"Damn it. I should've gone to the doctor with you. I knew I should've gone to the doctor with you. Didn't I tell you? There are all these things going on and I'm just finding out now. It's so. Damn it. Why don't you talk to me, Buck? You never tell me anything. Sometimes I feel like we're strangers. I think we should go to counselling like Barry and Deepah. I really do."

"The idea of going to counselling depresses the hell out of me," I say.

"We really need groceries, Buck. There's nobody in the house to eat. And we're just about out of saliva. You know what I'm like when I don't have saliva for my morning coffee. I don't think either of us wants to go through another scene like that."

"If I have to go to counselling, I'll throw myself into some kind of really big grinder."

"A grinder, Buck? Really? Where are you going to find a big grinder? It sounds to me like you just don't want to go to counselling and you're using your depression as an excuse. What'd the doctor say you should do?"

"He gave me a prescription."

"A prescription? Oh God, Buck. A prescription makes it seem so much more real. Now I'm worried. I need a prescription, too. The fact that you're depressed and I love you so much and I try so hard to make you happy just makes me want to cry. I don't know what to do, Buck. I really don't. What'd you have for lunch?"

"I got an arm from the vending machine," I lie.

"I don't know what to do."

Neither do I, but I say, "I'll be home in a little while and we'll go get groceries."

I end the telepathic call. If my wife wasn't already dead, I'd probably kill her. That's what I realize after I talk to her. I don't know why I stay with her. She loves me. I know that. I love her too, but I also hate her. I don't know if I love her more than I hate her or if I hate her more than I love her. I just know I hate her. When

I say "I love you" to my wife when we go to bed at night or when I leave for work in the morning, I'm telling the truth. But I don't say, "I also hate you. Possibly as much as I love you. Perhaps even more." When I say "I love you" I'm telling the truth, just not the whole truth. So help me, God, okay?

Zombies believe God is a supernatural creature. If God *weren't* a supernatural creature, so the zombie thinking goes, God would help us lay waste to supernatural creatures and infect the living people they protect but God won't. However, God doesn't seem to really help supernatural creatures and the living people they protect too much, either. Sure, supernatural creatures have all kinds of amazing magic powers, and, yes, living people get to die, which is nice, but living people suffer terribly pretty much the whole time they're alive. Zombie philosophers argue that the pain—spiritual, physical, or both—that living people experience while alive only makes the good feeling of death feel even better later. Otherwise, God would be a real jerk. The zombie philosophers aren't too sure why God set up the world like this in the first place but they're sure God has a good reason. Most of them. Pretty sure.

I hear Fairy_26 turn off the shower. I imagine her stepping out, grabbing a warm fluffy towel, and drying herself just as I imagined killing her and eating her. In my mind, there's no difference. Does she dry her wings with a towel? Or does she air-dry them by fluttering them? She probably uses a towel. Otherwise she'd get water all over the bathroom. I don't know for sure. I can't ask.

In the corner of my sightless white eyes, I see her. Stiffly, I turn toward her. She's standing in the hall, holding a white towel in front of herself. It loosely hangs down from where she holds it with one flat hand over her breasts. "Everything okay in here?" she asks. Her wings open and close, slowly, like a butterfly warming itself on a branch in the sun. Her green hair is dark and heavy with wetness. It's gathered in wavy clumps.

I groan.

"I'm just going to get dressed. I'll be right out."

I try to nod. It doesn't really work. She turns to go before I can decide whether or not to look, so I look and I see her perfect bare backside. Then, unsure whether I'm glad I did or sad I did, I turn and stare off into the distance, in my mind separating her and her world from me and mine. It's an unbridgeable expanse. No one even thinks of trying. It's the one certainty in this game of chance: everyone loses. What the hell am I doing here? I have a zombie wife. I have to take her to buy zombie groceries. I start getting up.

That's when Fairy_26, barefoot, comes dancing out of her bedroom wearing a short baby-blue backless dress from which her wings spring and spread and suddenly begin to flap in a blur when she sees me struggling to get up. Her naked feet lift off the floor. She flies to me. She hovers in front of me, holding out her small and alive hands with a look of concern on her sweet face in front of which strands of damp green hair hang. She takes my outstretched hands, gnarled like tree roots, in her soft flexible ones, supple like newborn leaves. Her beating-near-the-point-of-invisibility wings flap even faster as she flies backwards, pulling on me, helping me off the sofa. I almost think I feel what it's like to be alive again, through her, through touching her, or more precisely, through her willingness, no, her eagerness to touch me, but it passes as soon as I recognize I'm just feeling something, anything other than the numbness, the sadness, and the dead-heart racing despair of being who and what I am, and who and what I wish I wasn't. When I'm standing upright, Fairy_26, still hovering, still holding my twisted hands, says, "Okay?"

I grunt.

She pouts. "Do you have to leave now?"

CHAPTER THREE

The Illusion Of Difference

I shake my head to say, "No." I forget all about leaving Fairy_26's tree branch apartment as soon as she helps me up. I fall back onto the mossy cushions of the sofa like I'd only stood up because a lady had entered the room and I'm polite.

Hovering before me, Fairy_26's wings slow. She descends and lands lightly. As she stands there, looking at me, trying to figure me out, her wings open and close, wide open and tightly together, in slow, peaceful way that looks like it feels incredibly satisfying, like a good stretch when you're human and you wake up first thing in the morning, completely rested from a good night's sleep and you're so alive you feel like you could do anything even though you couldn't. She catches me staring at her wings.

"I know," she says. "They're strong for such fragile-looking things."

Neither of us says anything for a long time after she says that and I wonder if we're both thinking about living people, about being living people, about being strong and looking fragile, about being fragile and looking strong, about the two of us meeting under different circumstances, less complicated ones, or if it's just me.

"You might be the perfect man," sighs Fairy_26. "You listen and don't say anything." She brushes at something invisible on the front of her dress, on the façade, the lie. "Sorry again about that scene in the store. It's my fault. I should've known better than to get involved with an elf. At first, it's all singing and dancing in the forest and everything is wonderful and then you catch him getting it on with some bitch by a stream. I hate naiads. They're sluts. I shouldn't say they're *all* sluts. Most of them are sluts. They're usually gorgeous but this one wasn't even that beautiful. I don't know what he was thinking. I guess he wasn't. Men." She harrumphs. Then she remembers me and says, "Sorry. I didn't mean you."

I point at my head and move my hand away quickly, like I don't think either and she laughs. It makes me so happy: seeing all these things happening quickly, her calm ocean blue eyes widen and her pretty mouth open a little and turn up at the sides, exposing her perfect teeth and her pink tongue, and watching her body shake with glee. Only a fairy can feel glee. I'm convinced of it when I see her laugh. When she laughs, she laughs completely. Even her wings laugh. They shake with her body. After a time that passes too quickly, Fairy_26 settles down. She smiles at me for a while. Then she looks away. Something heavy and hard inside me falls and thuds.

"Usually I go for giants," she says, sitting on the mossy floor about five feet in front of me. "Before the elf, my last two boyfriends were giants. I like the brooding type, I guess." She's sitting on her left hip. Her left hand is flat on the natural carpet beside her, supporting the light weight of her upper body. Her slender legs are together. Her knees are bent. "Generally, giants have depressive personalities. Like you," she says, glancing at me. "Depressive personalities, not depressing," she adds, peeking at me. She laughs again. The laugh turns into a smile. The smile slowly fades. She frowns. "Giants don't like the way they are, either. They wish they were normal-sized. They're loners. I like loners: people who don't fit. It's probably because I don't feel like I fit, either. Maybe nobody does. I don't know. I don't think it matters." She rubs her right calf and I don't think of all the things I'd do to experience what those fingers feel because I know it'd take several especially long eternities. "I used to sit in a giant boyfriend's ear and talk to him." With the same hand she used to touch her leg, she finger-combs her a freshly fallen clump of damp green hair behind her ear. The sunlight turns her hair into millions of different shades. It's brighter in some places and darker in others. Where the sun puts its shape-shifting hands on her directly, it looks almost white. Fairy_26 touches her ear. "Not right inside his auditory canal. That'd probably tickle. I'd lay on the fleshy ledge just beneath it." She shows me, smoothing her finger over that orangey-pink indented part of herself, just above her earlobe. Then she pulls her hand away. "He'd wander the countryside. I'd talk. His name was Troublemaker but he wasn't a troublemaker at all. He was big, though. Talk about a tricky love life. Boy. I tell you."

She lapses into silence then, leaving me to think about it. To imagine it. Are giants sized proportionally?

"I think that's why I usually go for giants," says Fairy_26. "Because they're sad." She plays with the hem of her baby-blue dress, staring at it. "I like to make people happy. I don't know if I ever do but I like to try." Without looking at me, she shrugs. When she does, the spaghetti strap on the right side of her dress slides off her right shoulder and falls against her right arm. Desperately, I try to communicate with her telepathically but in an anonymous way so she doesn't know it's me, to ask her to leave it there, but she hooks it up with her thumb and lifts it back into place. "Maybe it's because I think if I make someone else happy, I'll be happy then, too, because I'm really *not* happy but I think I'm happy enough. I told you I cry and cry sometimes but I don't feel sad all the time. Really. I swear." Tucking both legs beneath herself, sitting on her heels, she holds up her hand, swearing to me. Then she lowers it. "Anyway, I still miss Troublemaker sometimes."

I moan.

"What happened?" she interprets. She shrugs. "What always happens?" Suddenly her wings blur into motion, lifting her off the floor. When she's at precisely the right height to stand, her wings stop. Her feet touch down so gently it's like they were never off the ground. She walks over to her music player. "Do you like music?" She looks back at me over her shoulder.

I nod and nod. Zombie music all sounds the same to me. It's sexual and rhythmic, the way human and supernatural music is, but zombie music is made up entirely of human screams, zombie groans, and the sound of things breaking and I get enough of that at home.

She turns on a song. At first I think it's an orchestra of instruments but then I realize it's a choir of voices. Fairy voices. They sing the wind whispering through spring leaves and gales crashing into winter cliffs. They intone a small fire crackling in dry fall branches and a raging inferno roaring through a hot summer forest. The room resonates with the clicking of stones and the tumbling of boulders. It's the union of all things. The harmony of the universe. It's all one big bang, breaking everything apart, perfectly, so it can be alone. Without us. Within us. It's the sound of the supernatural, which is so natural it can't be understood or accurately described. It can be reproduced, but why? Why isn't it good enough as it is? The song Fairy_26 plays for me is the sound of everything people and zombies aren't. "Do you like it?" she asks, swaying to its beat, turning to me.

Dumbly, I nod.

"Dance with me."

Awkwardly, I try to get up. She flies over and helps. When I'm standing and I seem steady enough, she lands in front of me. "Okay." Concentrating on the problem, she puts one hand on the back of her head. She ruffles her green hair. It's still drying. "How are we going to do this?"

She moves in such amazing ways. Her elbows work; her knees bend. She curls her toes in the soft moss carpet. She smiles. She tips her head from side to side, cheerfully.

When she stops playing with her hair, her arms hang loosely at her sides, not rigidly out in front of her. She's so alive. I try not to stare at the pulse beating in her neck. I try not to think of the blood and meat of her beauty. She's constantly recycling. It's such luxury, seemingly beginning again, with every breath.

I lower my outstretched hands onto her shoulders. She moves closer. I'm so surprised I almost take a step back but I'm slow and awkward and I recover before I have the chance. She comes as close as she can, wrapping her arms around me completely. She holds me tightly. She presses the side of her beautiful face into my undead chest. My arms reach out above her uselessly, touching nothing, pointing nowhere.

"I'll help you a little," she says. Her wings turn invisible, fluttering. She lifts me a few inches off the ground. She begins moving us in time with the music. She knows this song. She knows every bend and curve and dip and swell. She hugs the music as tightly as she hugs me. After I get over the surprise of it all, I can almost feel it. I can almost feel her. I can almost feel the fairy voices and the sound of everything. For a second, I understand the smallest part and the whole and how there's no difference, just the illusion of difference. Just as the vast majority of humans can't see the zombie world or the supernatural world, I've been unable to see the one thing I ever needed to see and as soon as I look at it, directly, I can't see it anymore but even when it disappears, I remember what it looks like. I don't know if I'll ever see it again but I know I'll spend every second searching and I won't forget who showed it to me. It's so fast but so important. I can't believe I'm still dancing with Fairy_26. I can't believe she didn't stop and say, "You see?" But she doesn't know I did and I don't know if she ever has.

Briefly, I wonder if she slipped me something, some sort of hallucinogen, or if the perfume of her hair is intoxicating me but I don't care. It doesn't matter how or why I saw what I saw; I saw it. What am I going to do when I find it again? Will I worship it or destroy it? Is there any difference? No. Just the illusion of difference. I have to remember that. I repeat the words in my head, over and over, while Fairy_26 holds me off the ground and moves me to the music of everything she knows so well.

"Have you ever heard of Guy Boy Man?" she asks.

CHAPTER FOUR

Farm-Raised Humans Don't Taste As Good As Free-Range

My zombie wife, Chi, and I are at the grocery store. I'm pushing the cart. It has a waist-high horizontal handlebar. It has four wheels. It has a metal cage into which you stuff the bodies of living people. The cage is six feet by six feet. It has locking gates on either side for your convenience. There's also a smaller, easily accessible, non-locking cage on top for smaller items such as fresh brains, saliva for your wife's coffee, and that kind of thing.

The fact that I'd never heard of Guy Boy Man excited Fairy_26 so much we had to leave her tree branch apartment right away. Holding me by the hands, she flew me from downtown Fairyland, over fields of flowers too beautiful to dream: irises, poppies, peonies, and violets. Laughing, she swooped down right above them and dropped me into them. They were enormous. Each flower was as big as a large room. I'd slide down the silky petals. I'd bounce down the velvety ones. I'd land in the soft centre. Awkwardly, I'd stand among pistils and stamens that were taller than I. The colours of the flower were so bright and sharp it hurt to look at them directly. I could see them with my eyes closed.

In the middle of a tulip, Fairy_26 showed me Guy Boy Man on the inside of bright whiteness that stretched up and curved over us, like it was protecting us. Guy Boy Man was ecstatic, brandishing the Pope's hat, waving it at us, like we were the Pope or he knew the Pope would be watching and he kept saying, over and over, "I have your hat!" Fairy_26 explained to me who Guy Boy Man is. I guess he's a real superstar in the supernatural world. Guy Boy Man is a sixteen-year-old pirate and spiritual leader who may have, inadvertently, caused a global financial crisis in the process of becoming unspeakably wealthy. He actually likes to talk about it but it turns out not many people want to hear about it.

Anyway, Guy Boy Man is one of the very few humans who can see zombies for what they are. With his vast resources, he's managed to expose a number of zombie banks and zombie institutions. Currently, he's in the process of rallying others to his cause, which is to end human suffering. Fairy_26 explained Guy Boy Man's odd clothing choices. To reflect his role as spiritual leader, he wears a shiny, high-tech, white, plastic ceremonial robe. To indicate he's a pirate, he wears a pirate hat. Apparently, Guy Boy Man pirated the Pope's pirate hat—the tall gold and white one—and now it's Guy Boy Man's pirate hat.

In the tulip petal, Guy Boy Man wielded the Pope's hat like a weapon and said, "It costs ten percent of your weekly salary to belong to the Pope's religion. For a limited time only, if you go to www.howtoendhumansuffering.com, you can join *my* religion at the low cost of *nine* percent of your weekly salary. "That's a savings of one percent every single week! There are fifty-two weeks in the year. It's simple mathematics. Just by switching from the Pope's religion to mine, you'll save *fifty-two percent a year*!"

In the grocery store, my wife and the mother of my son is tearing up the list she made. She's knocking items off shelves and down onto the floor. "I do the best I can, Buck," she says. "I don't know what else to say. I love you with all my heart. I look after you and our son. Are you happy? No. You're depressed."

"It's not your fault, Chi. It's a chemical imbalance."

The aisles are wide enough to permit two carts to pass each other going in opposite directions.

"It's a chemical imbalance," she scoffs. "I know that. You know that. But that's not what *zombies* are going to think. You know what zombies are going to think? Zombies are going to think there's something wrong with *me*." She mocks, "'If Buck is depressed, things must be great at home. His wife probably keeps the house too tidy. I bet she cooks. Maybe she's lousy at having sex in human blood and filth in front of horrified people she and Buck haven't eaten yet.' Oh God." She turns to me, scared. "Is there something wrong with me, Buck? You'd tell me if there was something wrong with me, wouldn't you? Is there something I do that you *don't* like? Is there something I could do that you *would* like? I'm not talking about cleaning the house, taking a bath, or washing my clothes, Buck. Because that's not happening. Okay? That's just me. If you don't like it, well, I don't know what to tell you. Too bad. Tough luck. Be depressed."

"You're not doing anything wrong, Chi."

The Pope and spiritual leaders of other organized religions are among the most important human beings with whom zombies have alliances.

The busiest and noisiest section of the grocery store is the "Fresh Meat" section.

When Fairy_26 and I left the tulip, I considered, mindlessly, how upsetting the Pope might upset the zombie hierarchy. I'd never knowingly encountered anyone from the upper echelons of the zombie world but I always assumed there was an upper echelon and it kept things going. Fairy_26 flew me to a stream where we landed on a twig that floated on the surface tension while the clear water below became a clear picture of Guy Boy Man ranting:

"Zombies ruin the environment and they want *us* to fix it? Forget it. Not me. I turn on all the taps and I leave them on. I buy regular light bulbs, not those dim little compact fluorescent pieces of crap and I turn them on and leave them on, day and night and I don't have a smart car. I have a big, dumb-ass American bulldozer. And I leave my big, dumb-ass American bulldozer idling all the time even when I go to bed at night and in the morning, I get up and I don't need to turn on any lights because they're already on and I shave, shower, and brush my teeth but I don't need to turn on the water because it's already pouring.

"I get dressed in cheap clothes made by sweatshop kids because sweatshop kids need money too and I go out to my big, dumb-ass American bulldozer, get in and I don't have to turn it on because it's already running and I drive it uneconomically—speeding up to red lights and peeling out when they turn green—to the gas station and I fill 'er up.

One day, when the tank is full, I'm going to keep pumping. I'm going to pump until gasoline rivers run down all the streets in the world. Then I'm going to light those rivers on fire because fire is awesome. I'm going to watch the flames dance and the black smoke fill the sky and I'm going to laugh and laugh and laugh . . ."

Right now, Chi and I are in the "Frozen Foods" section where a zombie can get a TV dinner consisting of an unidentifiable cut of human flesh along with a dollop of artificial mashed potatoes and a rather pathetic looking serving of vegetables. There are also rows of frozen human legs and arms hanging on hooks behind glass doors that hiss a little when you open them, and spill out a cold wind over your lower undead extremities. The corners of the glass are usually covered with frost. Behind other glass doors, there are hands and feet sitting on shelves. For budget-conscious zombies, there are whole frozen torsos available that you can take home, thaw, and de-bone yourself. For those with a little more money to burn, individual frozen cuts are available: lungs, livers, kidneys, hearts. Nobody buys frozen brains. It just isn't done. Sure, you could probably ask the butcher and, I suppose, he'd go along with it if you gave him a long explanation of why you want a frozen brain but who would? You want your brain fresh. Aisle Four.

Chi pulls a couple of human arms from the freezer. "I know you don't want to hear this, Buck," she says, sticking the arms into our cart. "But we need marriage counselling."

"You need marriage counselling," I say. "I don't need marriage counselling."

"Buck, all our friends are going to marriage counselling."

After we left the stream, Fairy_26 brought me to a tree that filled the sky. It had more leaves than I could see and we landed a long way from it. Fairy_26 told me it was as close as we could get. She said it was as close as anyone or anything could get. It was an important tree. I wanted to get closer. I needed to get closer. Fairy_26 knew it. She picked me up and flew me toward it and even though the rest of the world sped by in a blur, the tree stayed the same distance away. Was it retreating? Were we just not advancing? On the leaves of that tree, I could see Guy Boy Man and in my mindless mind, I could hear his words:

"I want to make a brief point about the futility of everything. I know that sounds like it's going to be depressing but it's not. Really." He paused, thinking about it, looking up at his own eyebrows. "Okay it's going to be a little depressing," he admitted, finally.

He paced back and forth but the leaves always showed his face or the side of his face and there were times I knew he was gesturing with his hands even though I couldn't see. "Here's my brief point about the futility of everything: it's not for us. All the work we're doing: the sky we're scraping; the inroads we're supposedly making. It's for other people. People we've been told, lead to believe, convinced, will be around after us. We're actually trying to make the world easier and better for people we'll never even know. And we'll never be done. And we'll all die trying. To do something we don't understand. For people we don't know. And all that'll be left of us, any of us, when we're dead and gone, will be a pyramid, in one form or another, a testament to nothing and no one, a monument proving only our slavishness, ironically, to something which never had any real power, a shrine to the suffering we never needed to endure, but for which we volunteered ourselves, and worse, our children."

"Fine," I volunteer. "If it'll make you happy, we can go to marriage counselling."

"Really, Buck?" says Chi, guiding the front of the cart into the chaotic "Fresh Meats" section while I push it. "Do you really mean it? You're not just saying that? Because I think we really need marriage counselling. I think we're going to discover we have a lot of problems."

CHAPTER FIVE

Unhappiness

Here in "Fresh Meats," you have your choice of free-range or farm-raised people. The free-range put up a fight *and* they're delicious. That's what most zombies want. So, of course, free-range people cost more. Farm-raised humans are annoyingly docile *and* they lack that free-range flavour. That's the general consensus. Some zombies prefer the milder taste of the farm-raised people but most zombies want the free-range zest and tang. Of course, almost all zombies derive sexual pleasure from the fight put up by the free-range ones but it's rarely discussed in polite society and zombie society is, if nothing else, polite.

"Pardon me."

"Not at all. Entirely my fault."

"You're too kind."

"I'm so glad we're going to marriage counselling," says Chi, directing the front of our cart into the path of an oncoming cart. We collide. "It's the right thing to do. Everyone will agree. Your depression is a symptom of an underlying problem. You and I need to root around in all our pent-up resentment and unspoken bitterness until we figure out what's wrong. Resurrecting all our petty arguments, reanimating the problems we never solved, giving new life to our differences and how incompatible we are is key."

"I feel better already."

"Oh yeah. We're going to talk about your sarcasm *a lot*."

The zombie into whose cart Chi directed ours has pulled hers back. She stands there for a moment, not thinking. Then she starts ramming her cart into ours, over and over, mindlessly. She wears a heavily stained tailored black pantsuit with no blouse. Her exposed skin is mottled grey-white. Her unbuttoned jacket reveals her bare breasts every once in a while when her cart crashes into ours. Her dirty blond hair is stuck up with every kind of filth unimaginable. Her white eyes see nothing. Everything is infuriating in them.

When she withdraws her cart to slam it into ours again, I move our cart to the side, safely out of the way, while she's out of position. She propels her cart forward as if nothing has changed. When she fails to collide with anything and, instead, her cart moves forward easily, she loses her grip on it and it goes rattling away. She falls to the floor.

Chi and I move on.

ZVFFA

Here in the "Fresh Meats" section, they, the naked free-range human beings, shake their cages and howl with animal rage. They curse and spit. They fornicate. To entertain themselves. They try to urinate on you and defecate on you. Like zombies care. Filth and wounds are signs of zombie prestige. In any event, when you pick a person you want to eat, you open their cage, reach in with the store-provided taser and you shock them.

When they're incapacitated, you reach in, grab them with both hands, and pull them into your open cart. You close and lock the cage from which you got them, along with the gate on your cart. Then you move on. It doesn't take long at all. Without the taser, it'd be hours of sweaty, bloody, screaming work, pulling out the free-range ones. The farm-raised ones, on the other hand, just climb into your cart when you open their cage. You can shock them if you want but there isn't much point. It's easier to just let them walk into your cart. If you shock them, you have to drag them into your cart. Some zombies shock them, wait for them to recover, shock them again, wait for them to recover again, over and over, mindlessly, and they wind up blocking the aisle.

Before she brought me home, Fairy_26 flew me to the sky and in the huge blueness there, behind small scattered white clouds that looked like freckles on his face, I saw Guy Boy Man, and with a thunderous sound, he spoke:

"You know what makes the world go around? It's not love. It's not money. It's *unhappiness*. It's *dissatisfaction*.

55

Think about it. Misery is the reason for everything. The only reason to create anything, or, in the unusual case of God, everything, is because you're dissatisfied. You don't waste your time creating something else if you're happy with what you already have, right?

"From the moment you're conceived, you're unhappy. You start dividing, trying to get away from yourself, trying to escape. You can't. You scream your way into the world. As soon as you're old enough to realize that unhappiness is your problem and crying isn't going to get you everything you ever wanted, you start hoping, foolishly hoping, the miserable feeling will pass. Being a kid sucks so you spend all your time wishing you were grown up. You think you'll be happy then. You believe it. You're sure of it. When you can drive, everything will be great. But it isn't. When you can leave home, everything will be great. Then it's not. All of a sudden, you're grown up and being a grown-up sucks too! Being a grown-up might even suck worse than being a kid! When you grow up or, more accurately, think you should have grown up by now, you start to panic a little. Why are you so *miserable*? Maybe it's because you're single. Being single sucks. So you try dating. Dating sucks so you try marriage. If you're a woman, you probably *dreamed* about getting married and then you had kids because being married wasn't as great as you thought it'd be and then you went back to school because having kids wasn't that hot either and then you had an affair. If you're a guy, you probably got married because you met a girl you were more afraid of losing than you were of getting married to and you had kids because your wife wouldn't shut up about it and then you locked yourself in the office until you could have an affair. Maybe you're gay, which I've got to believe is almost always ironic or you're alone, which is great except for the loneliness.

"Nobody is happy. Nobody is satisfied. Basically you just stagger around your whole life, not knowing where you come from, not knowing who you really are, not knowing where you're going and doing things you hate because you think you wanted to at some point or you think it'll lead to something you want at some point. You didn't and it won't."

Fairy_26 told me Guy Boy Man has a prayer:

"God,
The world sucks;
It's a real mess;
Nobody can fix it;
It's hopeless;
Thanks a lot;
Amen."

"You know what we should talk about at marriage counselling?" I ask Chi, not confrontationally, but completely un- and disinterestedly. I'm not sticking up for myself anymore. I don't have the strength or I don't care. I can't tell the difference. I'll go to marriage counselling. It's just another thing to feel miserable about. I'd add it to the list if I had the energy to make a list.

"This should be good," says Chi, sarcastically. She tasers a plump naked young woman who was backed into the corner of her cage, holding out her hands like, "don't." "Okay, Buck, I'll bite. What should we talk about at marriage counselling?" Chi opens the woman's cage and drags her into the aisle. "Wait a minute," says Chi, dropping the woman, straightening up, and looking down at her. "She's dead."

"Must have been the taser," I observe.

"Don't be ridiculous," scolds my wife, looking at the corpse, expressionlessly. "Tasers have never been linked to any death conclusively."

"You think all the deaths they've been linked to inconclusively were coincidences?"

"I *don't* think, Buck. All right? You might want to give not thinking a shot. You're a zombie. Not thinking would probably help a lot with your depression."

I leave the back of the cart, lean down, pick up the plump girl and stick her back in her aisle cage. When I close the cage door, I notice everybody is looking at me. All the zombies pushing carts full of screaming people have stopped and are staring at me. I just cleaned up a mess. They're shocked.

"It's okay," Chi assures them, holding up her hands. "He's depressed. He knows what he's doing. It's not his fault." I shuffle back behind the cart and get it moving again. Chi stumbles up beside me. "You have to be more careful," she warns, telepathically.

"Marriage counselling isn't what you really want, Chi," I say.

"What do I want?"

"Something you can never have. Just like I do."

Before Fairy_26 left me right outside my front door, she said I could visit her any time I wanted. I could call her, too. She gave me two tiny packets to summon her: one of sleeping butterflies, the other of the powder to wake them. She said she'd sense the disturbances the butterflies make in the air. She smiled. My rigid arms were outstretched toward her. She was holding my right hand and when she let go of it, slowly, I watched her amazing fingers pulling down the length of my disgusting ones until she ran out of me. I watched her fly away.

Outside the grocery store, in the parking lot, a balding man has just finished bashing out the brains of a zombie couple who'd wheeled their cart to the back of their vehicle. That couple could have been Chi and me. The balding man has a crowbar. Breathing heavy from his exertion, he spots us. He stares at us, murderously. Even though the day is warm, he's dressed in layers, probably believing his clothes will offer some protection from zombie bites. He starts jogging toward us with anger on his face and fear in his eyes. He holds up his weapon, menacingly. With her arms outstretched, Chi staggers toward him, groaning, like a good zombie should. I stay behind. Two of the three people in the cart I've wheeled out shriek encouragement to the man making his way toward Chi. When he thinks he's close enough, the balding man swings the crowbar at Chi's head. He isn't close enough. The crowbar whizzes by Chi. When the man is turned to the side from his enthusiastic swing, Chi wraps her arms around him. In a brutally violent kiss, she bites into the side of his face, pulling out a mouthful of flesh, which she begins to chew. Blood covers both their faces. The man screams and screams, shaking and twisting, trying to break free of Chi's deadly hold. A small group of zombies exits the grocery store and stumbles toward me. "What happened?"

"Some guy with a crowbar was attacking zombies."

"Terrible. This used to be such a safe neighbourhood."

A minute later, when the group of zombies has joined in the parking lot feast, Chi, covered in blood and bits of flesh, ambles back to me. She pushes past me, to our car. She opens the passenger-side door and falls into the seat.

Without looking at me, she says, "Thanks for your help, Buck." Then she slams the door.

CHAPTER SIX

All Human Children Are Born Of Zombies

On the way home from the grocery store in our brand new eco-friendly vehicle, with one naked caged male in the back, fists clenched around the bars, white-knuckled shaking them, spitting threats, one naked female screaming at the top of her lungs, and one naked young woman sitting silently, holding her knees to her chest, rocking back and forth, trying not to look at the cuts of human meat lying all around her—the loose arms and legs, the plastic-wrap-covered hearts and livers in white-plastic trays—it seems Chi and I aren't talking anymore. Even though we're speeding dangerously, destined to crash, only to have a brand new eco-friendly vehicle waiting for us in the morning, courtesy of the supernatural creatures with whom we, the zombies, have an arrangement, I see it close-up, in perfect detail, as I race past: an abandoned stuffed animal in the gutter. A lion. It's been there for a long time. It's been exposed to the elements. It's dry now but it's been waterlogged so many times it'll never look dry again. I feel like that. The strange thing is, I don't want to go back for it. I want to leave it there. It's where it belongs.

What am I going to do? Give it a good home? I don't have one.

All human children are born of zombies. Of course, the children don't know their parents are zombies. Children can't see us for what we are. The supernatural creatures hide us, how we look and sound, from the young, to protect their developing brains from the brutal and hopeless reality of their existence in our non-care. Supernatural creatures enable our young to understand our words so we can lie to them. We tell our children everything will be all right. We tell them stories about supernatural beings and we tell them they're lies. We tell them lies about the world and tell them they're the truth.

There are two reasons: we need the workforce to help us destroy and we need the food to help us spread the destruction. Zombies are expansionists. We don't know where we're expanding and we don't know why. We just know we are. Should we be?

Why do the supernatural creatures help us do this to our children? The truth is, we don't really know. We *believe* it's because of their love for human children who don't become zombies; human children who grow up to be mentally ill prisoners, unsuccessful artists, and that kind of thing.

Z V F F A

Earlier, when Fairy_26 told me Guy Boy Man killed forty zombie teens, almost singlehandedly, at his high school this morning, I knew exactly what she was talking about: the riot in maturity section. Barry Graves told me about it this morning at work. He said heads were rolling. I wasn't interested then. I wasn't interested in anything then.

I'm interested now.

After I crash into the neighbour's front porch, get out, wave to them through the front window and Chi and I get the groceries inside, she asks me a question I've been dreading since Fairy_26 brought me back to her: "What do you want for supper, Buck?"

Constance, the cat, slinks up to me. She moves so easily. I can tell she takes her effortlessness for granted. She doesn't think about it. She doesn't thank God for it. Her speed and agility will always be there when she calls upon them. She doesn't fret. About anything. She doesn't wonder if she's loveable. She rubs against my leg and expects to be petted. She stands there—so poised, elegant, and confident—looking up at me, expectantly. When she finally realizes I'm not going to bend over for her, she walks away. Then she stops, turns back, and glares at me. I hate that cat.

"Buck, what do you want for supper?" Chi asks again.

I don't know why I'm not hungry. The thought of eating nauseates me. Is it because I'm depressed? I don't know. Maybe I'm just sick of all the arguments over meals.

"Do you want me to gnaw off a thigh for you, Buck?"

"I can look after myself, Chi. Thanks."

"What are you going to have?"

"What does it matter?"

"I want to know what *I* can eat."

"Eat whatever you want."

"I don't want to eat something you're going to want later."

"I'll eat whatever is left."

We're having this conversation wordlessly, facing each other, standing in the locked and padded room where we keep the people we're going to eat. The screaming woman is screaming. The catatonic girl is huddled in the corner. The angry male is punching me as hard as he can. I can't feel it.

"You're such a martyr, Buck. Just tell me what you want."

"I don't want anything right now, Chi. I'm not hungry."

"What do you think you'll want when you *are* hungry?"

"How am I supposed to know?"

"That's a big help, Buck. Thanks."

"Why does it matter so much?"

"Why? I'll tell you why. You know what's going to happen? I'm going to eat the last heart. Half an hour from now, you're going to ask me if I ate the last heart."

"So? So what if I do? So what if you did?"

"You really don't get it, do you, Buck?"

"No, I don't, Chi. Why don't you explain it to me?"

"If you don't get it, I don't think I can explain it to you."

The angry male quits punching me. He takes my head in both hands to crash it into his knee, to try to bash out my brains. I stop him. I push him away, easily. I watch him fall. I look at him as he slips, slides, and finally gets up off the blood, excrement, and urine covered floor. He stares at me, breathing hard, with his fists clenched. I don't know if he truly wants to kill me or if he just wants to live. Is there a difference? I don't know. For a reason I hate and don't understand, I don't let him end my torment.

"Don't eat the last heart," I tell Chi. "Problem solved."

"It isn't about the last heart, Buck. We have lots of heart. It's about *consideration*. It's about *respect*. It's about *give and take*. It's about *communication*."

"Tell me what you *don't* want. That's what I'll have."

"I don't want that. I want to know what *you* want."

"I don't *know* what I want, Chi."

"Just don't think about it for a minute."

"I want this conversation to be over. That's what I want."

"Just tell me what you want!"

The angry male falls to his knees, crying big clean saltwater tears. He weeps, knowing there's no hope, there's nothing he can do, he's a prisoner, he's going to live this nightmare until he dies as nobly as he can.

"I want the catatonic female," I tell Chi.

"Really?"

"Really."

"I was going to have the catatonic female."

"Fine. Have her. I'll have the screamer."

"No. I'll have the angry male. You have the catatonic female."

"It doesn't matter to me, Chi."

"You haven't been eating properly. I want you to have whatever you think you can stomach."

"Now who's being the martyr?"

"I'm not doing it because I feel sorry for myself. I'm doing it because I care."

"Okay. I'm sorry. Thanks, Chi."

"After I eat, do you want to make love in front of the two horrified survivors?"

I don't. I really, really don't. But I don't want to talk about it. I don't want to talk about *why* I don't want to, nor when I think I *might* want to, nor what I think my not wanting to *means*, both about my physical unwell-being and in terms of my relationship with Chi. I don't want to talk about how it makes *me* feel, how it makes *her* feel, and how we aren't *discussing* it properly.

"Sure, Chi," I say. "Sounds good."

I don't know how or why at the beginning of our relationship, when I wanted sex and she didn't, there was something wrong with me. I was some sort of horny weirdo. Now, when she wants it and I don't, it doesn't mean she's a libidinous freak. It means I don't love her. It *says* something. About us. Our relationship. I don't care enough to point out the inconsistency. If I did, she'd just talk, talk, and talk until I agree with whatever she's saying, however she's saying it.

"You have it wrong, Buck," she'd say, even though I don't. But I don't have the strength, energy, or the patience to stick up for myself. I don't want to talk anymore. I'll do anything. I just don't want to talk about it. As Chi staggers toward the hopeless male and the screaming woman screams louder than ever and the catatonic girl goes away somewhere even farther in her mind, I try to leave the room. Even after I leave the room, I try to leave the room.

CHAPTER SEVEN

Word Came From On High

The next day at work, I sit at my desk, pondering everything I learned about Guy Boy Man, a living boy who can see us, who recognizes us for what we are, and who wants to destroy us. He has the enthusiasm of youth. He has the wherewithal of wealth. I'm excited. I *want* him to destroy us. I want him to destroy *me*. I never thought someone else would do it. I'm so tired. I don't have the energy to destroy myself. I don't have the strength. Aside from Guy Boy Man, everything else I can think of saddens me. He's a speck of gold in the dark cave of my life. Is he fool's gold or the real thing? Does it matter? I'm a fool. I'll take what I can get.

The thought of Fairy_26 saddens me.

Before I met Fairy_26 and heard the sermons of Guy Boy Man, I just did my job. I destroyed senselessly: mindlessly; religiously. I picked up my paycheque and went home.

Some days, after work, I went out marauding with my colleagues. We'd crash a mall or an airport. It was mindless entertainment and an excellent source of vitamin human. But now, I don't know what to do. I just sit at my desk, trying to think.

Barry keeps stopping by, every chance he gets. For some reason, he's watching out for me. He's trying to encourage me. "You have to do *something*, Buck," he whispers. "You haven't done anything all morning. They're going to start talking. Just break a pencil, for God's sake." I don't know if my wife talked to Barry's wife and Barry's wife told him to do this or if Barry is doing it on his own. Barry looks around, making sure nobody is watching and he spills a can of tomato soup over my head. It's like he genuinely cares instead of just going through the motions of caring, which is what zombies usually do.

Barry comes to my cubicle, hiding a Molotov cocktail. He looks around, confirming that what he's about to do will go unobserved. Then he lights the Molotov cocktail, throws it against the wall and yells, "Good one, Buck! Wow! Look at that sucker go! You guys see what Buck did?" I don't trust Barry. He's good-looking. Maybe he's having an affair with my wife. It wouldn't surprise me. That's the way my life is going. Marriage is a sacred institution. That's why divorce is illegal. So my wife is contractually obligated to remain faithful to me until someone bashes out our brains but infidelity is pretty much typical zombie behaviour. It isn't typical for me, though. I honour my commitments.

Maybe that's my problem. The thought of ditching Chi and Francis Bacon and trying to start something with Fairy_26 hasn't crossed my mind once. It's crossed it so many times it's just about covered up everything else. I honour my commitments, though. I keep telling myself that.

A legless zombie drags itself and the chewed off ends of its legs, which trail dreadlocks of meat and sinew, to my cubicle. The legless zombie informs me that the director of this branch wants to speak with me in the conference room. The legless zombie drags itself away. Uninterested, I watch it go.

Overhearing, Barry stumbles to my side. He gives me a pep talk as I struggle to my feet. "Lift your arms," Barry says. I didn't even notice my arms aren't outstretched. I've been holding my arms out for so long, reaching out for peace, or love, or the capacity to understand anything and to warn me if I'm going to run into trouble, I can't remember what it feels like not to do it. It feels like this. It feels good. I just stand there for a moment with my arms down. Then I lift them. I don't do it because I want to. I do it because I don't want to hear Barry tell me again. I'm so sick of people telling me what I already know and repeating themselves when I ignore their words.

Barry ambles beside me as I stagger toward the conference room. "This is it, Buck," says Barry. "I know you're not feeling like yourself but these are troubled times and you don't want to wind up on the street. You have a wife and family to consider." He thumps his arm against my back, encouragingly. "You have to dig deep, Buck. You have to pull out all the stops. It's now or never. It's do or remain undead. You have to put on a zombie *clinic* for this supervisor! Buck, you can do it! You *have* to do it!"

"Okay," I say.

In the conference room, the director is sitting in a big chair with his arms outstretched in typical zombie fashion. He's wearing a suit jacket but he's not wearing a shirt. Numerous gunshot wounds are visible in his flabby torso: black holes in the grey space of his upper body. A knife gash splits the side of his face, exposing the rotten purple meat of him. The very top of his head is bald but filthy. The hair he has on the sides is short and brown but dark with congealed human blood and it's styled chaotically with it. He's missing his right shoe. His right sock remains and it remains bright white like it was freshly laundered. It's such a shocking breach of zombie etiquette it almost sparkles and glows.

As soon as I wobble into the conference room, I grab the mini-projector and throw it on the floor. It doesn't break. I lurch over to it. I stomp my foot down on it, over and over, until I'm sure it's wrecked. Then I overturn the conference room table. When I finally sit down, the director tells me, enthusiastically, "You really tore this place *up*, Buck!"

"Uh huh," I say, dispassionately, like I tear it up all the time.

"No, I'm serious," says the director, seemingly impressed. "You wrecked it."

"I hate what I do," I say.

"And that," he says, pointing a finger at me. "You always know the wrong thing to say."

"I'm not a team player," I say, shrugging. "I don't know how many times I can say it. I hate working with others. If I could get rid of all you jerks and do this crap myself, I would, believe me, but I need you losers to mess up the stuff I don't have time to get to personally. I believe in slowing things down. Lowering productivity. You know what our problem is?" Stiff necked, I twist in my chair to look at the director, sweeping my outstretched arms through the air. "Efficiency. We're too efficient. It's bad for the economy. You know why? We can't hire more workers. More workers equals paying out more in salary. Paying out more in salary means a smaller bottom line. A smaller bottom line is good for America. Why? The more jobs we create, the more ancillary jobs get created. The zombies with new jobs can afford to buy the stuff we don't make to break for themselves and they can afford to pay income taxes instead of just being a drain on zombie society."

"You're really on the ball, Buck," says the director, shaking his head with his glazed white eyes wide, apparently in awe.

"I have suggestions, okay?" I try to crash my hand down on a table that isn't there. "I have ideas. On how to fix this place so it causes even *more* damage. This place operates too much like a well-oiled machine. We need to throw a little sand in the oil. We need to create *problems*. You know why? Because problems are opportunities for solutions. If there's a problem, we can start a committee to look into it. The committee will assemble, gather evidence, compile a report, and give us a presentation. Then we'll understand the nature of the problem. We'll throw money at it. We'll hire experts in various fields. We'll actually hire experts to stand out in farmers' fields. They'll accomplish very little out there but experts need employment, too. We'll shuttle the data out to them. That's good for the shipping industry, which is really suffering in this high-speed information age. The experts will examine the data slowly, painstakingly, wandering around in farmers' fields. While they're doing that, we'll hire a bunch of ethnic zombies who'll work for cheap to actually *do* the hard work of separating the sand from the oil in the well-oiled machine. When the well-oiled machine is operating at maximum efficiency, which is bad, we'll throw a wrench in the works and start all over. That's how it goes. You know that. That's why you're the director of this branch."

The director nods, mindlessly. "Buck, we want to offer you a promotion."

"I don't want it," I say. "I really hate it here."

"You don't need to sell yourself anymore, Buck," says the director. "We're already buyers. Okay? We're buyers of you."

"This is terrible news," I mutter.

"It's all right, Buck," says the director. "You can cut it out now. I'm depressed, too."

Is this a trick? A trap? I don't want to walk into something. I don't want to fall into anything. I've lost my desire to survive but the instinct is in every undead cell of me. "What are you talking about?"

"You're depressed. I'm depressed. The whole upper management of this place is depressed. What, you think regular zombies operate this place? They would've run it into the ground a long time ago. No. Depressed zombies are in charge." As if to prove it, he drops his arms on his legs. "We keep things devolving at a certain pace. It used to be a great job but I'm afraid you're coming on at a rather uncertain time. If we were having this conversation a few months ago, I would've said, 'Buck, here's the deal. We have a board of directors. They don't do anything. Nothing at all. For this non-service, they don't earn an absurd amount of money but they get it. They employ people like you and me to do their jobs for them. We oversee ourselves. In return, they expect us to receive an absurd amount of money, too. In fact, they expect us to demand *more* money than they don't earn because they're not doing anything and they assume, wrongly, we are. Don't worry that this will be difficult. It won't. Far from it. It'll be a lot easier than what you've been doing until now. However, like I said, you'll make a lot more money in exchange for the lessening of your workload. It doesn't make sense but it makes sense if you don't expect it to make sense. The more money you demand, the more valuable the board will assume you are. So demand a lot.' That's what I would've said a few months ago. These days though." The director shakes his head. "Nobody knows *what* is going on. I'm glad you're joining us, Buck, but when I learned you were joining our ranks, I actually made a couple of calls because I couldn't believe we were bringing in somebody new. We've been making a big show of tightening our belts. It seems we're making an exception in your case." The director points at the ceiling. "Word came from on high."

"How'd you know I'm depressed?" I ask. "I thought medical records are supposed to be private."

"Would it surprise you to learn your wife told a few of her friends?"

"No."

"Okay, Buck." The director tries to stand. His rolling chair rolls away from him. With a small earthquake I feel under my feet, he crashes to the floor. Out of habit, his arms stretch straight up toward the ceiling. He curses. He rolls over and starts getting up. "God, I hate myself," he mutters during the process. "All right, Buck. Let's go. I'll show you to your new offices. Don't worry about your personal effects. I'll have someone clear out your desk and bring everything up for you."

"I don't have anything I want to keep," I say.

"Really? Not even a blood-splattered shattered-glass picture of your wife and kids?"

CHAPTER EIGHT

Who's Using Our Brains?

Two hours after I settle into my new offices, the director rushes to see me, looking terrified. It takes a lot to terrify a zombie so I'm instantly alarmed. My offices are so tidy: no human body parts anywhere. There isn't even any blood. There's a disinfectant smell: chemicals scented like lemon. I keep thinking: supernatural creatures have been here; fixing, cleaning, organizing. Now the supervisor is here, destroying my ease.

"What is it?" I ask, awkwardly trying, and failing, repeatedly, to get up from my luxurious chair.

He ambles over, carrying a piece of paper. He drops it on my desk. It's an artist's representation of Fairy_26. It's a very good likeness. I hate it. I want to tear it to pieces. She's so beautiful. I despise the thought of other zombies seeing her, admiring her, passing her around, in painting form, destroying her with their stupidity.

If I could feel anything other than emotion, it'd make me sick. I'd feel hot, prickly. I'd turn to the side. I, a wretch, would retch. But I couldn't vomit. I haven't eaten for days. I never got around to the catatonic girl. Nothing came up.

The director stares at me, gauging my reaction. Then he turns away, grabs a chair for himself, pulls it closer to my desk, and sits down.

"This is a problem, Buck," he says, tapping the work of art.

I can't think of Fairy_26 as a problem. She's a solution. She's the answer to the question of why there are questions. If it was death before, it's she for whom my arms reach out now. Not her body. I can't bear the idea of exposing her to me any more than she has been already. But I love her. I know this now. Looking at the artist's representation, I know I love her. I love her more than I love my wife because my relationship with Fairy_26 isn't real. It's a fantasy. I could never be with her. She deserves so much better than me, a zombie. Besides, I'm contractually obligated to remain faithful to my wife until someone bashes out our brains. And I don't know if anyone is good enough for Fairy_26. I love her so much. I actually want to help her to search for him, her, it, whatever or whoever it, she, or he is: the person, being, or thing who or that will make her happy. Can anyone make someone else happy? Can anything? Is this what Guy Boy Man means? I've given up trying to be happy and now I want to make someone else happy, someone who might never be. Is it all a trick to keep us going? Working? Is it all pointless? "How is this a problem?" I ask.

"They *know*, Buck," says the director, panicked, gesturing at the painting. "They know about *her*."

"Who does? How?"

I'm not sure exactly what happens. I get the impression the director wants to tower over me, dramatically, but his legs fail him so instead he just falls forward out of his chair, hitting his head on the edge of my desk. He gets up. He starts ambling around my offices, seemingly disoriented. What's the matter? Is it the collection of antique clocks on the shelves? Is it the historic maps showing the world with different borders? Is it a concussion accompanied by memory loss? "This is crazy," he says, finally. "Everything is falling apart."

"But that's good, right?" I don't know why I want to be optimistic all of a sudden. The director's fear has spread to me. I'm more afraid than miserable now. I suppose if I had time to think about it, I'd wonder if there's much of a difference. I might suspect that if I were afraid for long enough, I'd become miserable and if I were miserable for long enough, I'd become afraid of that which I'm capable of doing: to stop it; to stop it. The strain. "We're zombies, right? We like chaos. The more disorderly, the better."

"Sure, we like chaos. Look." The director grabs a golden telescope pointed out the floor-to-ceiling windows. He turns it to the side and lifts it and its stand over his head. He stumbles away from the windows, toward the wall opposite. Then he hurls the telescope and its stand. "I'm throwing something against the wall and, what do you know, it makes a hole and I think that's terrific but that's not the way things work."

"Of course it is." Why am I arguing? Why do I want to cling to the world I loathe? Why am I scared of mayhem unravelling? "Destruction is key," I insist. "That's the zombie code. Nobody understands why we live by it, but everybody benefits from it. Destruction leads to reconstruction. Wrecking and rebuilding the same things, over and over, leads to innovation: new and better ways of performing necessary tasks. Using your example: Somebody makes the telescope you threw. You bought it, broke it, and now you're going to buy a new one. It's good for the economy. Additionally, people will be hired to repair or replace what's been damaged. By punching a hole in the wall and, in the process, ruining the telescope, you created jobs. The unemployment rate dropped. The good news will be reflected in the stock market. Investors will be rewarded. Furthermore, the newly employed will need to buy tools and materials. Whoever makes those tools and materials will see an increase in sales. They'll hire more workers to keep up with demand. The new workers will have disposable income to invest or spend. Whether they invest it or spend it, it's good for the economy. And we put money into research and development every time we destroy something. People will either make it so the telescope you throw either doesn't create a hole in the wall, it doesn't break when you throw it, or both. People will develop ways to more quickly and more effectively patch any future holes caused by the telescopes you throw or anything else for that matter. People will ultimately render themselves completely unnecessary and there will be no jobs at all because things will run so smoothly and then the future will be destroyed because it will all be pointless and that's what we want, right?"

"Buck, Buck, Buck," sighs the director. He taps his finger against his temple. "They're in our heads. Our *heads*. We only use *ten percent* of our brains, right? Who uses the rest? *They* do. They control us. They show us what we see. They tell us what we hear. They make us do their dirty work for them. We're powerless. They let us think we're in control."

"Who does?" I gasp.

"That," he says, pointing at me, like I'd got to the matter of the heart, "is the right question to ask."

I think of zombie computers: powerless computers that do what other computers tell them to do: spread the virus. The strain; the strain. "Who's using our brains?" I cry.

"Albinos!" exclaims the director.

CHAPTER NINE

You Might Act In A Way Contrary To Your Best Interest

Neither of us says anything. Finally, because I'm completely and thoroughly convinced the director isn't going to speak until I do and because I can't think of anything else to say, I say, quite calmly, "Albinos?"

"They were just in my office," confirms the director. "We here, in upper management, have suspected for a long time there was a group of people, beings, or entities, maybe even a mix, in charge of us, because if there weren't, we, the zombies, would've ruined everything a long time ago. We didn't know who they were or what they wanted but we assumed we were on the right track because they never intervened. That's all changed now. They were in my office."

Again, because I can't think of anything else to say, I say, again, "Albinos?"

"They have very white skin and hair."

I struggle to remember what little I know about albinos. "They have pink eyes, too, right?"

"They were wearing sunglasses," says the director.

"Inside?" I say, shocked.

The director nods like, "I told you so; they were albinos. Inside," he says.

"Wow."

"I know."

"Okay." I have to admit it. "It sounds like you had albinos in your office."

"That's not the scary part."

"It gets worse?"

"One was a movie executive and one was a record industry rep," blurts the director, in a torrent.

I gasp. I can't believe it. "I thought they were just a myth!" I cry.

"So did I."

In horror, I stutter. I sputter, spit, and mutter. Then I manage to expound: "A bugaboo. A campfire story. Something you tell kids just to scare the hell out of them."

"They're real," says the director, paler than usual. "I saw them with my own undead eyes."

"Give me a second."

"Take your time."

I don't pause at all. "Were they alive or undead?"

"I don't know. I couldn't tell. But I know this much. They were thoroughly unappealing. Revolting. I'd never eat anything like that. You could pay me . . . I don't know how much. I wouldn't do it. I couldn't."

This is a nightmare. I can't wake up. Movie executives? Record industry reps? I look out the floor-to-ceiling windows, trying to escape reality. Across the street, in another office building, I see a group of zombies in the process of shattering one of their own huge windows. Pieces of mirrored glass drop in deadly reflective shards. I watch as the zombies push a big mahogany desk to the broken window. The desk teeters on the edge for a moment, like it might remain. They push it more. It falls in a slow spin. The zombies stand in the opening, looking down, watching it go, and, presumably, shatter when it hits the ground forty-two storeys below.

"The albinos wanted me to talk to you, Buck," says the director.

"Why? Why didn't they come to me directly?" I'm relieved they went to him but I think I should know.

"Good question, Buck." The director retakes his seat on the other side of my desk. "I'm impressed. You're really overcoming your mindlessness. They came to me because they're unsure about you. You're depressed." He tries to comfort me. "It's not your fault. It's a chemical imbalance. The albinos actually caused it." He explains. "Depressed zombies serve a purpose. Apparently, it's the albinos' purpose. However they say—forgive me, Buck, I'm just passing this along—your irrationality makes you somewhat unpredictable. You might act in a way contrary to your best interest. You might, for example, attack them, in your fright. So they wanted me to talk to you because we know each other. We have a rapport, don't we, Buck?"

Something about the director seems suddenly desperate but I can't think that and I try not to even feel it because I don't want to reveal anything to the albinos in my mind. "Sure. We have a rapport."

"I know you probably don't trust me," says the director, like he's in my head, reading my thoughts, like an albino. "*I* wouldn't trust me if I came to myself with a story about albinos who control everything, including me. I'd wonder what the hell I was talking about. But there's this." The director motions at the painting of Fairy_26 on my desk.

I've gone from staring at it, at her, to trying to ignore her, it, the painting, and that which it represents, everything she is and means to me, so the albinos don't know that which they can't have possibly missed. Can they get at her through me? What can I do if my thoughts and feelings betray me? What hope do I have? None? "There's this," I admit, acknowledging the likeness of Fairy_26.

"They don't want you to put her in any danger," assures the director. "They know you won't. But they *do* want you to use her. I'm sorry, Buck. They want you to use her to get close to Guy Boy Man."

CHAPTER TEN

Think Of Zombies As A Whole

I let the director's words fall deep into the sinkhole of my depression; I let them burst on impact; I let them splash down and swirl around. I absorb them; they seep into my recesses. The albinos want me to use Fairy_26 to get close to Guy Boy Man. How do they want me to use her? Why do they want me to get close to Guy Boy Man? What are their plans? "Why should I go along with this?" I ask.

"Depression sure snaps you out of being mindlessly selfless, doesn't it?" remarks the director. "But I wish I could appeal to that side of you right now, Buck. Think of zombies as a whole. The albinos are really distraught over Guy Boy Man. Not only is he one of the few living people who can see zombies, he has an idea. Normally, the albinos love ideas. They buy them for cheap and use them to make obscene amounts of money. But Guy Boy Man isn't selling and his idea is contrary to all the other ideas the albinos have already purchased, used, and reused countless times. If Guy Boy Man's idea becomes much more popular, it could begin to unravel the fabric of our society."

I move my shoes on the wool carpet, trying to feel the floor. "We really do like chaos, don't we?"

"Absolutely," says the director. "But the *albinos* only like chaos when it appears orderly." The director sticks his hands on his bald spot, as if he knows he's in it up to there, over his head. "You have to keep in mind I'm new to all this, Buck. Movie executives and record industry reps don't show up in my office every day. I didn't even *believe* in them until two hours ago." He sticks his fingers into the congealed goo in the hair on the sides of his head and holds them there. The director looks at me through completely white eyes. "They're so scary, Buck. They don't take calls; they don't do lunches; they don't order in expensive coffees; they don't yell at flunkeys and lackeys. I wish I could forget them. I wish I could go back to consolidation. I *understand* mergers. I *understand* acquisitions. I make deals with or buy out the competition because competition is difficult and no one really likes it. It's the strain. It's too much work: innovating; improving. Trying, trying, trying." Realizing he's gone off on a tangent, the director takes his hands from his hair and stares at the disgusting mess. "We, the zombies, *don't* like organization, stability, and regulation but the supernatural creatures *do* and, unfortunately, we have to share the planet with them. I shouldn't say 'unfortunately.' It's in our own best interest. If we, the zombies, were able to, somehow, destroy supernatural creatures, we'd eat or infect all humans, including our own young while they're still too physically small to be of much food value and we'd plunder our people farms and we'd wreck everything before long, levelling all buildings, filling in all tunnels, and we'd run out of things to destroy eventually and it'd get really boring and we'd slowly starve to death, probably turning on each other near the end."

"You paint a pretty bleak picture," I say, not looking at the work of art on my desk.

"It's realistic. In any event, the albinos are concerned because we, the zombies, risk exposure by Guy Boy Man. Currently, irresponsible living people are discussing us with increasing frequency. The mainstream media refers to 'zombie banks' and 'zombie institutions.' Thus far, they've been doing it in a completely offhanded manner, most likely because the truth is so horrifying. However, even casual references are worrisome. As you know, currently, only a few living people, like Guy Boy Man, recognize us for what we are and these people, heretofore, have been unorganized. In the recent past, when groups of people learned of our existence and accepted it as fact, it was too late, because they were guests at a surprise massacre party. But if Guy Boy Man manages to convince large numbers of living people we, the zombies, exist, and are intent on turning them into zombies or, failing that, eating them, it'd be catastrophic for us. It'd spoil the meat, for one thing.

You don't want freaked out meat. You want it to be freaked out when you're just about to eat it and when you actually dig in but you don't want it to be freaked out the whole time it's alive or anything. That'd just make it tough. For another thing, we'd invariably start encountering pockets of organized resistance. As I'm sure you know, there already are a few groups of supernatural creatures intent on overthrowing zombies."

"I don't know anything about that," I say, quickly.

"I'm sure you don't," says the director, dismissively. "It's just that, apparently, the albinos have curtailed our zombie appetites just enough to prevent us from self-destructing. That's our natural orientation, Buck. Albinos are our super scary saviours.

There was a time when our appetite for living human flesh didn't matter in the grand scheme of things. There weren't that many zombies and there were lots of people so everybody was happy. Well, the people weren't happy. They were terrified, obviously. But the zombies were happy. At least, the ones that weren't depressed. Anyway, there were a few zombies, lots of people, etc. Then, all of a sudden—what do you know?—there were fewer people and lots of zombies. Alarmed at the stomach turning turn of events, supernatural creatures got involved. I guess they really went to town on us. When it became clear we, the zombies, were going to be wiped out by supernatural creatures, albinos intervened. They took control of our mindless minds. This is where the war proper, if a war can be proper, began. It's doubtful any zombie managed to inflict casualties before receiving albino assistance. Before the albinos got involved, zombie troops would, invariably, rush headlong into brain-bashing disasters. With albino mind-controlling help, zombies began employing military strategies. The supernatural creatures started suffering losses. The loss of even a single supernatural life is catastrophic in that community and the albinos were prepared to sacrifice huge numbers of zombies to inflict casualties on supernatural creatures. At a certain point, the supernatural creatures realized something had changed but they had no idea that 'something' was the albinos. They only knew we, the zombies, were no longer, at least no longer always, mindless. They didn't know what they were up against anymore."

"They were up against albinos," I sigh, wondering how anyone, or any group, could threaten or destroy a group of zombie-mind-controlling albinos, thereby threatening or destroying all zombie-unkind, including me, and the director. As if reading my thoughtless thoughts, the director nods. "They still don't know about the albinos. They only know a powerful group, like the albinos, must exist, and be involved. It doesn't matter. Actually, it does. It matters quite a bit. It's a valuable piece of information. I don't know why I said, 'it doesn't matter.' Wait. Now I remember. I wanted to get back to the history. Reluctantly, the supernatural creatures agreed to a truce, which they negotiated with us, or, rather, which they unknowingly negotiated with the albinos. Through us, the albinos struck a deal with supernatural creatures, in which we, the zombies, agreed, to our own benefit, not to eat all living human beings—all at once—and to infect only those living people who unmistakeably embrace the zombie way of life. In return, supernatural creatures agreed to hide us—zombies, for the most part—and our destruction—to a limited extent—from the living. Mostly the young, whom, as you're aware, we train to become future zombies, or, failing that, taste great. The truce continues to this dark day. Thus far, try as they might, and they definitely do, no ragtag band of supernatural creature revolutionaries has been able to reopen hostilities."

"Why would albinos interfere in a war between zombies and supernatural creatures in the first place?" I wonder, telepathically.

"Apparently, albinos use zombies as a work force and to forward their shadowy agenda. Buck, it seems you've landed in the middle of some serious political intrigue. The albinos tell me we're at a crucial point in one large-scale financial transaction. This deal wasn't supposed to happen now but it's been hastened by Guy Boy Man's theft of trillions of dollars from the global economy."

"Piracy," I correct.

"I'm sorry?"

"Guy Boy Man doesn't steal or thieve; he pirates." I have to be as honest as possible at all times. In my words and deeds. So the albinos in my head start to trust me. Trust is necessary for deception. I don't know how or when I'll deceive. I only know I will. I assume the albinos know that, too. But if I don't plan it, if I act spontaneously and until that time, I do whatever the albinos want and then in the future I act without thinking, which should be easy for me because I'm a mindless zombie, perhaps I can protect Fairy_26 and maybe even Guy Boy Man. "How did the albinos get so powerful?" I ask. "Isn't albinism a genetic mutation? I thought it didn't get passed on very well."

The director just looks at me for a while with blood on his hands. "Buck, they were in my office for less than two hours. We talked business. I don't know anything about albinism. I'm not a scientist. I didn't even know 'albinism' was a word until you used it. And I certainly don't know anything about their history."

CHAPTER ELEVEN

Why Does Barry Graves Care?

"I'm interested," I say, about the albinos' history.

"I'm sure they're flattered," dismisses the director, wiping his bloody hands on his pants. "Look, Buck. I don't need *albinos* to tell me Guy Boy Man is a problem. I'm mindless and I'm clinically depressed but I'm not suicidal. I have suicidal ideation but I've never acted on it. Anyway, we've been working on the Guy Boy Man situation for a while now. We've started committees, task forces, and working groups. We have lawyers working on it around the clock. Our communications experts are still looking into ways of subverting his message but Guy Boy Man seems to have foreseen every potential attack and he's set-up defences in advance. We thought we had him with hate speech but he says he doesn't hate people who belong to other religions; he just thinks they're bad, wrong, unclean, inferior, and, ultimately, doomed to the fieriest depths of hell. He said he's sure they feel the same about him and he's right. Additionally, he argues, making fun of the most deeply held and cherished beliefs of other religions, along with their rituals and traditions, is one of the most deeply held and cherished tenets of *his* faith. Game over. Man wins."

I look down at the shiny top of my walnut desk. In its gloss, I see the director. I wonder if he can see me in the desk too. Staring at the director in the polish, I reflect on Barry Graves, the good-looking zombie, the husband of Chi's best friend, Deepah. Barry and I aren't really friends. I suppose we get along as well as any two zombies whose wives are best friends but we're not close. He's been shot in the face, twice, and he's been handsomely burned. He's a real ladies zombie. He's always flirting with women in the office. I think about his concern for me: pouring tomato soup on my head; making it look like I threw a Molotov cocktail; giving me a pep talk before I spoke with the director. Why does Barry Graves care? Is he having an affair with my wife? Did he think Chi would leave me if I got fired? Was he worried Chi would pressure him to leave Deepah so he and Chi could be together? Why does Barry Graves care?

Why does anybody?

"Should we surrender?"

Would I care if Barry Graves and my wife were having an affair? Don't I want to get away from her and Constance and Francis Bacon? Don't I want to get away from everything of which they remind me? My surrender. To everyone else's happiness. And seeing how miserable we are despite my sacrifice. Staring at the director, the sparkling zombie in the glistening top of my desk, I wonder if the albinos have a way to resurrect us all.

"No," he says. "We can't. That's not an option. God. I can't believe it's come to this."

I look up at the director. "What, exactly, has it come to?"

"Albinos!" he exclaims, his face vacant.

"Right."

"A movie executive!" he cries, expressionlessly. "A record industry rep!"

"I'm sorry."

"It's okay," says the director, trying to regain his composure. "I'm just having . . ." He focuses. "We, the zombies, up to this point, have made no overt overtures to Guy Boy Man. We assumed he'd become one of us eventually. He'd become part of the system. He'd accept responsibility. But it appears Guy Boy Man doesn't take anything seriously. Even that in which he believes most deeply. That's what makes him so dangerous. He's completely unpredictable. He does whatever he thinks is most amusing. He could give it all up tomorrow or he could raise an army."

"He's a human teenager," I agree.

"The thing is," broods the director, "he wouldn't have to do anything differently. In public, he could rail against us all he likes. But in private, he'd accept our friendship. He'd stop ramping things up. He'd provide us with information every once in a while. We need intelligence. Already we've had reports of highly illegal black-market condom factories popping up."

CHAPTER TWELVE

Eau De Life

I see myself—my grey-white mask of an undead face—in the big TV in my offices. It's off. I don't know if it's turned off or if it's just not turned on but I'm here and, somehow, I'm in there. I'm in the TV. I'm in the darkness.

Before he left, the director said, "Ask me if you can have smaller, less ostentatious offices."

"I like these offices," I protested.

"Just ask."

"Can I have smaller, less ostentatious offices?"

"No," said the director, tipping over his chair to the side and tumbling out. It was as if he recognized there was no way to get up gracefully, so he might as well choose his embarrassment. Clumsily, he got to his feet. "Remember you asked me that if you ever get called in to testify."

As I think that over—alone now, in my offices—and how I, happily, get to see Fairy_26 again and I even get to speak to her in a language she'll be able to understand but, unhappily, I have to use her to get close to Guy Boy Man, to whom I'm supposed to offer an olive branch, which sounds okay, from my personal perspective because I won't be harming him physically although I'm concerned the albinos in my brain might take ownership of my body, possessing it, and force me to act in a way contrary to my will or that they might make it my will and I'm fearful Guy Boy Man will accept the olive branch, squeezing, intentionally or inadvertently, the oil from the attached fruit into his religion, diluting his beliefs or changing their flavour, possibly even poisoning them, infecting them with us and as I take note of the time on the collection of antique clocks in my offices, remembering my appointments with the marriage counsellor, mindlessly, I turn on the TV. I don't understand. Any of it. That's what it boils down to. That's the essence.

The commercial is on zombie TV all the time. It features living actors. The star is an expressionless man. He wears a black turtleneck sweater. His hair is slicked down; side-parted. At first, you don't see him. An attractive young woman pushes an adorable baby in a stroller. She and the baby enter an elevator. The doors close. She and the child are alone. After a moment, the attractive young woman sniffs. She makes a disgusted face. The baby starts crying.

The expressionless man starts to appear. It's as if he's taking his own elevator into the elevator shared by the attractive young woman and the crying baby. When he reaches their floor, he stops rising and stares directly into the camera. He whispers, "Life." Then he descends his personal elevator out of the other elevator. The attractive young woman never notices him. The baby keeps crying. The attractive woman just stares up at the elevator's numbers and how they get lit, so slowly, one after another.

Guy Boy Man says, "When you reproduce, you know, for a fact, your children will die one day, right? Legally-speaking, isn't knowingly, wilfully, okay, accidentally sometimes, causing the death of someone else called homicide or manslaughter? Isn't that morally wrong? When you commit homicide or manslaughter more than once, isn't that considered even worse? Now I'm not saying everybody who has children is a murderer. I'm implying it. Subtly."

In the commercial, the scene shifts to a stately living room. A handsome young man is holding the wrists of a beautiful young woman and the two of them are struggling against each other. "What *is* it?" demands the young man.

"I don't *know*," cries the young woman.

The expressionless man walks between the wrestling couple and the camera. With his body sideways to the camera, he turns his face toward the lens. He whispers, "Life." Then he walks out of frame.

Guy Boy Man says, "Condoms should be free and freely available everywhere."

"If you're against sex education, you're pro-abortion."

"If you're against birth control and sex education, you're personally responsible for starvation, disease, and wars."

On TV, a naked man and a naked woman hold each other, tenderly, beneath a sheet. Suddenly the woman scrunches up her face. "Oh my god. Is that . . . ?" She and her partner push away from each other, frantically. Beneath the sheet, the expressionless man slides between them, effortlessly. He's completely stiff. It's as if someone pushes him into view by shoving on his feet.

"Life," he whispers. He exits, as if someone pulls him away.

Guy Boy Man says, "Family values are zombie values."

The final scene in the commercial is a silent shot of "Life" perfume, in bottle form, sitting on a decaying body. The body has a leathery face drawn back into a soundless scream. The camera pulls back to reveal hundreds of bottles, sitting on hundreds of similar bodies, all of which are then, presumably, covered by big mounds of dirt sitting in front of the bulldozers that start their engines simultaneously and then the images, suddenly, stop. Lately the following white words have begun appearing at the end of the commercial on a simple black background: Now, New, Life, For Men!

CHAPTER THIRTEEN

Zombie Marriage Counselling

"You have to help us," my wife tells the zombie marriage counsellor.

"What seems to be the problem?"

"Him," says Chi, turning her outstretched arms toward me, accusingly. "He was miserable. He was crying all the time. He couldn't eat; he couldn't sleep. Our love life suffered. One night he even took a shower."

The zombie marriage counsellor looks up from her notes at me. Her undead eyes peer over the top of the shattered-lenses of her glasses. Then she nods. She goes back to jotting her notes. She's wearing a shapely skirt suit: black and white and red all over. All the news that's fit to wear; it's fabric made to look like newspaper; it's covered with blood. Blood is spotted on her face, too, drying in purple-black flecks. We're the counsellor's first appointment after lunch.

"I made him go to the doctor," continues my wife. "The doctor prescribed anti-depressants. I was so relieved. I thought we were going to be okay. But now he says he's not going to take them."

"Why not, Mr. Burger?" asks the counsellor, still writing. The ragged hem of her skirt ends just above her knees. Her legs are crossed but the one on top has been lopped off in a messy diagonal cut several inches above her foot. The wound dangles long thin meat noodles. Between the strands, I can see sharp white bone.

"I can't see the point," I say, with a shrug.

The counsellor's office has been trashed and trashed again. Chi and I are sitting on a love seat. The cushions are gone. The stuffing has been pulled from them. The formerly white filling is now bloodied and strewn everywhere, like gauze in an emergency room. Right now, all the rooms in my life are emergency rooms. I keep thinking about the albinos in my head. "There are albinos in my head," I announce.

Chi frowns at me, expressionlessly.

"I see," says the counsellor, feigning indifference. "And do the albinos in your head talk to you?"

Wait a minute. I didn't want to announce there are albinos in my head. Did the albinos make me do it? How am I going to get out of this? "Yes, the albinos in my head talk to me," I say. "But they mumble." I put my finger to my ear and pretend to listen. "I'm sorry? *Who* do you want me to kill?"

Without changing her face, the counsellor smiles, politely.

"Please, Buck," sighs Chi. "Now is not a good time."

Are the albinos actively involved in this counselling session? Are they telling Chi what to say? Are they telling *me* what to say? Are they making me wonder about them right now? Why? For what purpose? Toward what end? We use ten percent of our brains, right? I still have that ten percent, don't I? So, at most, I'm ten percent myself. I have to find that part and hide there. Until I can, I'll sit on the exposed springs of this ruined love seat, staring at its exposed bloody innards and the empty skins of its cushions on the floor.

"Our sex life," whines my wife. "It's killing me. I've had to engage in the most taboo fetishes to get him even remotely interested."

"For example," prompts the counsellor.

"Cleaning. He wanted to watch me clean."

"I see. Clean yourself or . . ."

"God, no. Never. I'd never go that far. I just pretended to do a little dusting." She clarifies. "I didn't, though. Write that down." Chi straightens up in a futile attempt to see what the counselling is recording. "I never actually dusted anything. I'm a decent zombie. Okay? I'm not some sick-o like Mr. I'm-Just-Going-To-Jump-In-The-Shower over here."

"Let's keep the name-calling to a minimum, please." The counsellor white-eyes my wife disapprovingly. She turns back to her notes.

"Doctor," implores Chi.

"I'm not a doctor," corrects the counsellor.

"I love Buck," says my wife. "I really do. But I can't unlive like this. I'm seriously thinking about leaving him."

"So you're at a crisis point in your relationship."

"That's right." Chi is, unmistakeably, impressed by the counsellor's assessment. "That's it exactly." She turns to me, nodding. "A crisis point."

"What about you, Buck? You've been very quiet through all this. How do you feel?"

"Depressed. I feel depressed." I shrug. "Aside from that, terrible."

"But you won't take your anti-depressants?"

"No."

Peering at me over the top of the shattered lenses of her glasses, she says, "Do you want to be depressed?"

"No, I want to be patronized."

"I'm sorry, Mr. Burger. I offended you."

"No, you didn't. I'm too depressed to be offended."

"I assure you, Mr. Burger, I only want to help."

"Do you have a magic wand? Can you cast a spell to fix everything?"

"No. I don't have a magic wand and I can't cast spells."

"Then how do you propose to help? Because I don't know how to convince you, either of you: The problem *isn't* that I'm depressed; it's that everything is depressing."

Resigned, I let my white eyes explore the office. I see the dark holes punched into the walls. I imagine the blind, mindless rage that caused them. Or the accidents. Or the accidents that led to the fury. I see the bloody handprints streaked down our walls.

"I'm not a supernatural creature, Mr. Burger," acknowledges the counsellor. "I can't make the world the way you want it. I can't take you to Fairyland. But I *am* a good listener. I may be able to provide you with insight, to assist you through this turbulent time." She starts kicking her footless leg, up and down. It swings long purple meat strings. "Your wife is in considerable distress over the state of your relationship. How does that make you feel?"

"Depressed. Pretty much everything makes me feel depressed."

"See?" says my wife, nodding. "This is what I have to put up with."

"Are you ready for your marriage to end, Mr. Burger?" asks the counsellor.

"I stick to my contractual obligations," I say.

"I don't know you very well, Mr. Burger . . ." starts the counsellor.

"You don't know me at all," I interrupt.

"But I sense a sort of disconnect with you, like you feel very detached, removed, withdrawn, from this situation, and perhaps even with non-life in general."

In a weary way, I look at the lamps knocked off desks and tables. I stare at their undersides. I examine the undecorated bases that support them. They're horrible. "You sense it? In addition to *not* being a doctor are you also *not* a psychic?"

"Buck," chastises my wife.

"I just don't know how many things a person can claim not to be, while, at the same time, pretend to be," I say, despairing. "I sense a sort of disconnect with you, counsellor."

"This isn't about me, Mr. Burger."

"No, of course not," I say, jadedly. "Why should it be? I don't know anything about you but I'm sure my wife, Chi, who always thinks everything through, examined your credentials, compared your education and experience to other counsellors, listed and explored the pros and cons of dealing with a counsellor versus going other routes and ultimately made the best decision, concluding you, from the pantheon of available alternatives, would be the best suited to help us. Or, I don't know, maybe her friend Deepah recommended you."

"Do you have a lot of pent-up hostility, Mr. Burger?"

"I wouldn't say it's pent-up."

"Why are you angry?"

"I think my wife is having an affair."

"What?" cries Chi.

"I think you're having an affair with Barry Graves." I say it calmly, without looking at her.

"That's ridiculous."

"You're having an affair with ladies-zombie Barry Graves from my office and you only want to have sex with me all the time because you're worried I'll become suspicious if you don't make yourself readily available."

"That's the craziest thing I've ever heard," dismisses Chi. "I'm not having an affair with Barry Graves."

"Then who are you having an affair with?"

"I'm not having an affair with anyone!"

"Mr. Burger," interjects the counsellor. "When people feel guilty about something, sometimes they project their thoughts, inclinations, or behaviours onto others. Is it possible that's what's happening here?"

I can feel Chi examining me. If her suspicion was a plant, it'd be documented with time-lapse photography: its back would burst through dark soil and it'd emerge in the foetal position. It'd orient itself. Then it'd stand up quickly, throw wide its arms, and open its flower eyes at me.

"No," I say.

"Is there something you want to tell me, Buck?" asks Chi, dangerously.

"No."

"Is there something you *should* tell me?"

"I just want to feel alive," I confess.

"Feeling alive, Mr. Burger," says the counsellor, "is unnatural. It's abnormal."

"Are you having an affair?" demands Chi.

"Of course not." I turn to my wife. I look at her unblinking white eyes. "I'd never do that to you, Chi." I say it sincerely.

"If anxiety over infidelity were removed from the equation, where would that leave your relationship?" ponders the counsellor.

"I don't know," I admit. I tip my head at Chi. "She's the one who's thinking about leaving."

"Only because the Buck Burger I knew, fell in love with, and married, seems to have left me already." Chi turns to the counsellor. "We tried to make love last night but he couldn't." Chi turns back to me. "Do you know how that makes me *feel*?"

"That might be a medical problem," intercedes the counsellor.

"Great," says my wife. "Another prescription he won't take."

In the counsellor's office, a bookcase has been tipped over. It's been lifted away from what it held. The books are everywhere. The pages have been torn out. Shredded. The lies have been mixed in with other building materials. Broken bits of wall have been pulled from their holes and crumbled onto the floor. In what remains between the openings, all the wallpaper has been scratched away. It's been pulled and peeled off. It's made new designs on the wall. The torn pieces of wallpaper are mixed up with bloody gauze: the stuffing pulled from the love seat. All of this was done with a passion I'm not sure I ever knew.

"I love you, Chi," I say. "But I don't love you the way *you* want me to love you. Is that my problem or yours?"

"It's *our* problem," sighs my wife. "I'm just scared it's too late. For us."

"We were so much in love," I tell the counsellor. "When we became zombies, we thought we could be together forever." I throw up my hands. "Look at us now."

"Undead people change, Buck," says Chi.

"We're supposed to be together forever!"

"I think maybe we have been, Buck. I really do."

CHAPTER FOURTEEN

The Biohazard I Am

Even though it looks like rain, I decide to walk to the pharmacy where Fairy_26 works. I have some thinking to do. I've been mindless for so long. The thought of thinking is exhilarating. It's probably so exciting because I finally have something new in my life. It's not just the same old things with my Francis Bacon and my wife. Chi is always on my case about spending more time with Francis Bacon. "He needs his father," she says. I still have a hard time believing it. She's talking about me. I'm his father. Francis Bacon is fifteen now. I wonder if he's heard of Guy Boy Man.

The religion is "awesome." That's what you put if you're filling out a form. If there's a spot where you see "religion" followed by a colon, you just write or, more likely, type, "awesome." If someone ever asks you which religion you belong to, you don't say, "awesome," because, as Guy Boy Man says, "That'd be weird." Instead, if someone asks you which religion you belong to, or, more rightly, which religion belongs to you, you say, "I'm awesome." The faith is known as "awesome-ism" and its adherents are known as "awesome" or, alternatively, as "awesome-ists." This is a bunch of technical information that runs through my head while I'm trying not to think of my fifteen-year-old son, Francis Bacon.

I've never sat him down, looked him in the eyes, put my hands on his shoulders, and said, "You weren't my idea, Francis Bacon." I've never done that for a number of reasons. Firstly, it'd be cruel. And secondly, I'd have to talk to him. I'd rather not talk to him. I *do* love him. He wasn't my idea and when I learned he'd be entering our lives, screaming and bloody, it would've turned me hot with fear if I hadn't already been a zombie. But I wanted this. That's the scary part. I wanted him because his mother wanted him and I loved his mother so much I would've given her anything she wanted. So I wanted Francis Bacon very much. I love him. Francis Bacon isn't the source of my unhappiness. He isn't the root of my sorrow. I don't know everything he's done but I know he's innocent of this. He didn't cause my depression. The albinos did. Francis Bacon sits in his room. He studies. His mother and I worry. We ask him to turn up his music. We buy him violent video games and encourage him to play. We suggest he should sneak young girls into his bedroom, fool around with them, and, if possible, have safe-sex with them. "At least oral, Francis. At least oral." We leave wine coolers on his desk and tell him to offer it to the girls. We leave him boxes of black-market condoms. It doesn't work. Francis Bacon wants to be a zombie like me.

I don't know why. What kind of example am I setting? Can't he see I'm miserable? Why would he want to emulate me? Doesn't he want to be happy? I want to shake him and say, "Don't be like me! Do everything completely differently!"

He wants to get good grades like I did. He wants to go to the university I attended. He wants to *not* live. He wants to exist, merely exist, in eternal undead torment, like his old man. If I weren't so scared for him, I'd probably be flattered.

Chi wanted children so much. Then she had one. Now she's always on the go. Is she heading toward something? Is she running away? I'm not sure. But she's always moving. It's strange she wears business clothes. Sportswear would be more appropriate. Chi wanted to have a baby because all her friends were having babies so we had a baby. Francis Bacon. She was happy for almost two years or maybe she was just exhausted. It was hard to tell. It was hard to tell her to stop. She devoted herself to his existence, forgetting her own. She replaced herself with him. She replaced me with him in every way but one, thinking it was the only one I really wanted. Rolling away from me, immediately afterwards, like she'd just arrived and she couldn't remember the journey, she'd done it so automatically, she'd say, "Buck? The baby is too quiet. Go wake him up."

"Okay, Chi. Okay." I'd stumble to the baby's room, which the supernatural creatures kept so clean and smelling so fresh. I'd moan at the top of my lungs. "Wake up, Francis Bacon! Wake up!"

I still wish Francis Bacon would wake up.

Guy Boy Man is right: no one is ever happy. No one is ever satisfied. We keep pushing and pulling on something that isn't going anywhere. The strain. That's what infects us. That's what makes us zombies.

On my way to the pharmacy, I stumble past a burning house. I can't feel the heat but I know it's there. The thick smoke is black, tumbling up toward the grey sky. I amble past a car accident. The front ends of two green vehicles are mashed in a recycled plastic kiss. They've been abandoned in the middle of the street, like a sculpture no one understands or cares about but which was produced by someone that everyone says is very good. It's raining now but it's too late to put out the fire.

Happy is something no one can be. Happiness drives by, honking its horn, when you're walking in the rain, like I am now. It doesn't stop. Not like misery. Misery pulls over and throws open the door. Misery will take you anywhere you don't want to go.

I'm getting close now. To the pharmacy. Last night, when I couldn't make love to my wife, I thought about Fairy_26. I'd never tell Chi this but I thought about Fairy_26 when I was trying to make love to my wife.

I don't think it'd make Chi feel better that it didn't help. Fairy_26 is beautiful and I'm attracted to her but I can't expose her to the biohazard I am. I won't. That's what I keep telling myself. I won't, I won't, I won't.

CHAPTER FIFTEEN

Aircraft Carrier / Pirate Ship

I won't bore you with the details. I won't tell you how amazing it is to see Fairy_26 again or how incredible it feels to see, believe, no, to know, she's excited to see me, too. I won't go on about the formula or the music it makes.

I won't explain what it's like to have a gorgeous and kind green-haired fairy dangle you, a zombie, while the two of you whip over the ocean's water and waves and through its fresh air to Guy Boy Man's aircraft carrier / pirate ship. Now Fairy_26 and I are onboard, in a room, waiting for an audience with the sixteen-year-old trillionaire pirate. Two steely-eyed square-jawed soldiers keep automatic weapons trained on us. A few minutes later, Guy Boy Man breezes in. I'm awed and overwhelmed. I can't believe I'm in the same room as he. He's a saviour, a rebel, an enemy of the establishment: the zombies, albinos, and the Pope.

Guy Boy Man wears the Pope's tall golden white pirate hat, which he had pirated, making it his pirate hat, and out from under which Guy's crazy black hair now sticks; Guy Boy Man wears a ceremonial robe made of shiny high-tech white plastic. He blows past where Fairy_26 and I stand, at the back of the room, guarded by square-jawed steely-eyed soldiers, to the front of the room. As he goes, I see glimpses of what's beneath his robe: pirate breeches and a loose-fitting white linen shirt and, of course, a lot of handguns.

"Leave us," says Guy Boy Man, moving behind a podium, opening a bottle of whiskey, lighting a cigarette, and waving the soldiers away.

They lower their weapons and begin to go.

"That was a test!" cries Guy Boy Man, throwing open his hands, gawking at them, incredulous. "Never leave me! You're my elite soldiers!" Guy draws one of his shiny silver handguns, pointing it at me. "This dude is a zombie, right? I don't know if you're familiar with zombies, but zombies *eat people!*" He taps the gun's muzzle against his chest. "I am people." Guy shakes his head. "I don't want to be eaten by zombies." He gestures at me, again, with the gun. "Obviously, I have this dude covered. Okay? Don't get me wrong. I can take care of myself. I'm badass." Holding a whiskey bottle in one hand and with a cigarette dangling from between his lips, Guy waves at me with his weapon. "I could take him out no problem. Bang," he says, mocking the gun's recoil. "All right? Bang. I put zombies down. I do the same to suckahs, fools, and little bitches. I take them *out*. That's what I do. On a regular basis." He nods. "Pretty much all the time. That's what I do." He keeps nodding. "I'm not kidding." He stops nodding. He waves around his weapon. "Think of it from my perspective. I pirate trillions of dollars from the economy and, in the process, make a lot of enemies, a lot of whom are zombies. So I employ you. You're elite soldiers. I just want you to be around, pretty much all the time, except for when I'm being sexy with my hot young female followers, which is most of the time, so, for the most part, you guys can kick back and play video games. But in the rare instances when I'm not getting it on with hot young chicks, I want you guys—not that women can't be elite soldiers—to be around, pretty much all the time, at least when I'm on my aircraft carrier / pirate ship. While we're together, I want you to stress out a lot on my behalf. I mean, bang," he says, pointing the gun at me. "I've shot the zombie, right? Am I sweating? No. But now I have a pissed off fairy flying around the room, doing all kinds of dangerous fairy things. I could handle that, too. Seriously. It wouldn't faze me. But it'd be nice, since I *do* employ elite soldiers—I do, right? You guys are getting your cheques?—if you were at least in the room to see me kicking zombie and supernatural ass so you can tell tales of my heroics later on. Anyway." Guy Boy Man holsters his handgun and turns his attention to Fairy_26 and me. "What's happening?"

"Guy Boy Man," says Fairy_26, placing a flat hand on her chest. "It's an honour to meet you. My name is

Fairy_26." She wears strappy blue heels and a skimpy backless red dress. "I'm a supernatural creature." She gestures to me. "This is Buck Burger. As you can see, he's a zombie. What you can't tell just from looking at him is that he's a *depressed* zombie. He doesn't like being a zombie. I'm a fairy pharmacist. I met Buck when he came to the pharmacy to get a prescription filled for an anti-depressant. I became interested in him because I was unaware there were zombies who don't like being zombies. I thought all zombies liked being zombies or never really gave their condition much thought."

"I had reason to believe there might be a few who disliked their circumstances," Guy Boy Man states, drawing deep on his cigarette. "You see it in advertising sometimes: 'Keep Away From Children', 'Keep Out Of The Reach Of Children,' things like that."

He sighs a wispy blue-white ghost. "Did you know Ivory dish soap is 'Hard On Grease'? It says so right on the bottle."

"I never realized that," says Fairy_26, astonished. "That's disgusting."

"In any event," says Guy, "during a series of exciting adventures I can't be bothered to relate here, I learned a great deal about zombies and supernatural creatures." He takes another drag from his cigarette, refilling himself with smoke. "Your being a fairy explains how you breached my defences and gained access to my aircraft carrier, which is awesome. My aircraft carrier is awesome. The fact that you breached my defences and gained access to it isn't. Firstly, because my defences are supposed to be (pretty much) impenetrable. Secondly, because I hadn't really thought about supernatural creatures assisting my enemies, most of whom are zombies, in their efforts to derail my plans (it's just one plan) to end human suffering."

"We'd never assist zombies that way," insists Fairy_26, her wings opening wide in emphasis. "No supernatural creature would *ever* assist anyone intent upon harming you or thwarting your cause. You have the full moral support of all supernatural creatures."

"I don't know about *all* supernatural creatures," he says, lifting the whiskey bottle to his lips. "There are always the angels to consider." He drinks.

"Angels aren't real, Guy Boy Man," assures Fairy_26.

"They don't care," he replies.

"Guy Boy Man," says Fairy_26, ignoring that, "since you already know so much about zombies and supernatural creatures, perhaps we can tell something of which you aren't already aware."

"It's unlikely. I'm pretty aware."

"The zombies learned of my friendship with the depressed zombie, Buck Burger," explains Fairy_26. "Since they're so concerned about you and your efforts, they sent Buck here, with my help. The zombies want to make you an offer I hope you won't accept. In exchange for your assistance, the zombies will cease all efforts to foil your cause or cause you bodily harm. They'll also encourage all middle- and upper-class zombies to give your religion serious thought."

"I already have the middle- and upper-classes," says Guy Boy Man. "They're the ones who can afford black-market birth control. They're the ones educated enough to use it. I believe birth control, especially condoms, should be free and freely available everywhere. I'll settle for nothing less."

I groan. I'm so self-conscious. I'm dressed like a businessman who's rolled around in blood, excrement, and garbage. I probably also smell like that.

"Normally supernatural creatures can't even *begin* to understand zombie speech," begins Fairy_26, examining my expressionless face, to see if she heard me correctly, "but Buck brought me a complex formula." She turns to Guy Boy Man. "The formula is what convinced me to bring Buck to you; no zombie could've come up with it, no matter how focused and inspired by mental illness. At first, I thought it was gibberish." She frowns, remembering. "It contained blatant mistakes. But the mistakes were repeated: twice; three times; even, in one instance, four times in a row. That's when I realized it was music."

She smiles. "It was a chemical formula the likes of which I'd never even dreamed. I mixed the ingredients into a pill. I think the zombies intended for *you* to take it but I wasn't going to take that chance. I took it myself. Now I can understand what Buck says."

"What'd he just say?" I ask.

The room we're in is perfect for this. Almost everything is metal: military grey. On the walls hang pictures of war machines: fighter jets taking off from the aircraft carrier; fighter jets returning. A destroyer in the sunrise.

Through Fairy_26, I tell Guy Boy Man that zombies are slaves. In some instances soldiers. In all cases controlled. I tell Guy Boy Man about the albinos in our minds. The average person only uses ten percent of his or her brain. Who uses the rest? The albinos.

Guy Boy Man nods, lighting another cigarette. "I had a vision like this."

"You have visions?" gasps Fairy_26.

"Lots," says Guy Boy Man, casually.

"What kind?"

Guy Boy Man rolls the tip of his smoke in the ashtray, shaping it. "Different kinds."

"About what?"

He lifts his cigarette and waves it around, noncommittally. "Things."

I inform Guy Boy Man that the albinos in his mind can't control him yet because he's still a teenager. His hormones exert a positive pressure, forcing out all contagions like the strain. I speculate it's probably the reason why albinos forced zombies to agree to a truce with the supernatural creatures in the first place, allowing them to, for the most part, shield human life until it reaches a certain level of maturity because the albinos couldn't infiltrate those young minds yet anyway. And Guy Boy Man is so incredibly irresponsible. Irresponsible people are immune. The albino message overtakes me: It's unknown if Guy Boy Man will continue to be so reckless in thought and deed but if he does, he'll most likely ruin that which he seeks to control.

"Wait a minute," interrupts Guy Boy Man, puzzled. "Control?"

Through Fairy_26, I explain what the albinos believe: Guy Boy Man is merely trying to upset the balance of things; to gain control over it; so he can mine it for his own purposes.

"They can't imagine anyone would ever, genuinely, endeavour to end human suffering with no ulterior motive?" asks Guy Boy Man.

I hear my reply leaving Fairy_26's mouth; I watch her lips when they move; I catch glimpses of her tongue. She tells him what I tell her: even if someone were so altruistic, or so foolish, the hormone-addled and the irresponsible share at least one thing in common with the zombies and the albinos: greed. Sooner or later, the albinos believe, Guy Boy Man will join their side and soften his beliefs, or at least his expression of those beliefs, so human suffering can continue, allowing him to extract that which he wants from it: money, sex, self-esteem, power; whatever the case may be.

"I already have all that stuff and I'm still not happy," says Guy Boy Man, lifting the whiskey bottle to his lips.

There's always more. I tell him; Fairy_26 tells him. There's always more. There's a chance; there's hope.

"No," says Guy Boy Man, setting down the bottle. "There isn't." He sucks on his cigarette. He exhales grey into the grey room.

I'm running out of things to tell Guy Boy Man. I convey that, while I wasn't there in zombie, my director reported that one of the albinos who explained the situation and made these offers was a movie executive and the other was a record industry rep.

Fairy_26 is in shock; it takes her several seconds to recover. Guy Boy Man keeps saying, "What? What is it?"

When he learns the horrifying truth, Guy Boy Man masks his fear well but I know it's there. It has to be. It must. Who wouldn't be scared? Movie executives? Record industry reps? They're a pirate's worst enemies.

I'm glad Guy Boy Man won't accept any of their offers but I wish I could extend this visit. I like being near Guy Boy Man. I admire his confidence; his resolve. I know he's afraid but he refuses to give up. The visit can't last, though. It pleases me. Nothing that pleases me can last. I realize that now. I just have to hold on to these infrequent instances as best I can like I'm holding onto Fairy_26 now or I have to keep moving like all these fleeting moments.

When we leave the aircraft carrier, Fairy_26 looks down at me dangling from her arms and she asks me if I've seen Guy Boy Man's most recent sermon. I tell her I haven't.

She turns the sun, sitting like a ball of gold on the horizon, into the face of the young man I admire and the sound of the wind is replaced with his words. While I'm entranced by him and what he has to say, I can't help wondering how long the pill will last on Fairy_26. I can't help wondering how long we'll be able to talk.

Before we left, as a gesture of good faith on behalf of the albinos, I gave Guy Boy Man the location of one of our people farms to do with as he pleases. Having been recently employed in Reproduction Section, I know the information is accurate.

CHAPTER SIXTEEN

Trying Not To Want What I Want

Before the pill wears off, Fairy_26 and I sit in her tree- branch apartment and talk.

"It's not every day a fairy carries me out to visit a sixteen-year-old trillionaire pirate–slash–spiritual– leader on an aircraft carrier at sea," I say.

"It's pretty normal for me," she jokes, shrugging.

We're close to each other on the smooth wooden sofa that juts out from the wall and which is covered in soft green moss cushions. I'm not sitting as much as I'm tipped back.

My legs are straight. My arms are outstretched toward the place where the opposite wall meets the ceiling. My backside isn't touching the sofa at all. Fairy_26 lounges on the floor in front of me, sitting on one hip, with one arm propping up her light weight. Having changed when we returned, she's dressed entirely in white: white, knee-high, high heel boots, white leg-warmers, white thigh-high stockings, and a short, white, T-shirt dress. Her green hair and blue eyes almost glow. Segmented with black lines, like veins on supple leaves, her otherwise transparent wings stick out from slits in the back of her dress. They open and close, peacefully.

"I think Guy Boy Man likes you," I tease, looking at her from my gross white eyes.

"Oh, please."

"You can hover."

"All fairies can hover. Besides, Guy Boy Man has *hundreds* of hot young female followers. His gothic castle is full of them."

"You're different."

"You're married." She doesn't look at me when she says it. Suddenly she's frowning, picking at the soft moss cushions beneath us.

"I'm married." I mentioned it in passing, passing over the ocean, wondering if it mattered to her, wondering if it mattered to me. Now I'm trying not to look at her, trying not to want what I want, hating myself for being who and what I am, for being so weak, and so dangerous.

"Do you have kids?" she asks, glancing up at me.

"One," I say, nodding stiffly. "A son. Francis Bacon. He's fifteen."

Fairy_26 forces a polite smile. Her eyes turn back to the floor. She brushes the palm of her hand, back and forth, over the moss she'd been picking at a few seconds earlier. "That's the hardest part of being awesome. The idea of no more babies."

124

"They're a lot of work."

"That's what I hear."

"You'll meet somebody," I assure her, mindlessly. "You'll have babies. You're young. You have plenty of time." It strikes me as strange I'm saying these things when it goes against everything I believe. It's hopeless. We shouldn't reproduce. Why am I doing this? I'm encouraging her to have something I don't want her to have. I just want her to have me. Only me. Nothing and no one else. But I don't want her to have that. I want her to have more. I want her to have better. I'm worthless. I'm important only inasmuch as I've donated sperm—DNA spilled into the disgusting gene pool—and I'm raising a future zombie. I'm important only inasmuch as I work for the albinos, doing things I don't understand for reasons I can't remember, and inasmuch as I use what money I make to buy top-end consumer electronics, destroy them immediately, and go back to purchase newer versions that they made while I was gone. I want Fairy_26 to have everything she can't have. Me. Someone better to disappoint her. Lasting happiness. Babies that never grow up, that never die, that sleep through the night, that smile and gurgle through the day, that don't need to be fed, and that don't need to be changed: into zombies. Babies that can look after themselves when you're sick of looking after babies or when you're bored and you want to go out.

"I'm awesome, Buck," she says, smiling sadly at the non-flowering plants covering the floor, like she's having the same thoughts.

"So am I." I sit up. "So. What should we be doing?"

She shrugs. "Having fun, I guess."

"What do you want to do right now?" I ask. "What sounds like fun?"

"Nothing," she confesses.

I wrack my mindless brain. "What about music? What about dancing?"

"You don't want to dance," she says, frowning at the ground.

"You're right. I don't *want* to. I need to. I have to. I must!"

She laughs, glancing up at me.

"If I don't start dancing in the next couple of minutes, something terrible is going to happen."

"Like what?" Her wings blur into motion. She smiles at me. When she's hanging in mid-air, she rubs her hand down her leg, over the amazing patterns the moss made in her bare skin.

"I don't know. I'll turn into a movie executive and you'll become a record industry rep."

"That's not funny, Buck," she says, seriously.

"Okay, I went too far," I admit. "But we better start dancing."

"All right." She flies over to her sound system and starts it. Supernatural music pours out. I can almost feel it brighten the dead and dark parts of me.

CHAPTER SEVENTEEN

A Celebratory Ham

My wife wakes up at three in the morning and walks in on me eating the cat. "What do you think you're doing?" Her arms reach out at me in the zombie equivalent of putting her hands on her hips. She's wearing a ruined evening gown. Once it was shining golden fabric that moved like liquid. Now it's scraped and scratched. It's torn. The lustre is gone. It's coming apart at the seams.

"You wanted me to eat," I say, telepathically, with a shrug. "I'm eating."

"I didn't mean Constance."

I take a bite of cat thigh. "Well, I guess you should've been more specific."

"Don't do this, Buck."

Chewing, not looking up at her, I say, "Don't do what?"

"Don't make this about me."

After I swallow, I wipe my lips with the back of my hand. "I'm not."

"Yes, you are. You want to fight."

"You're the one standing there with your arms outstretched like your hands are on your hips."

"I'm a little disappointed," she admits, gesturing toward the screaming room. There's no screaming now. Just the sound of a woman's exhausted sobs breaking into a coughing fit. "After all, we just got groceries."

"I'm sorry, Chi." I lift the thigh to my teeth and tear off another piece. "I wanted something different."

"Why didn't you say so at the store? We could've bought somebody foreign or something." She points at the bloody mess on the table in front of me: the carcass. "Constance was Francis Bacon's cat, you know. He loved the stupid thing." Without doing anything differently, she stops pointing and glares at me.

With my broken teeth, I tear the last of the thigh meat off the bone. With my undead tongue, I push it inside my cheek. "It's not a big deal. I'll get Francis Bacon another cat." I suck the inside of bone, trying to get the marrow. Then I drop the thin white stick on the floor.

Chi turns away, with her arms outstretched, like they're crossed. "I don't know how you can be like this. You're so cold."

I don't know how *she* can be like this. *I'm* cold? She's thinking about leaving me. She tells a complete stranger she's thinking about leaving me. Fine. Leave me. Go ahead. Sounds great. I'll be free. What'll you be? Huh, Chi? Will you have what you want if you don't have me?

Grabbing one of Constance's remaining legs, I drag her body closer. "What do you want from me? You want me to care? I'm depressed, okay? I have a chemical imbalance. It's not my fault." I chew the cat meat I'd kept inside my cheek.

Still turned away, she shakes her head. "That's really convenient, isn't it? That's your excuse for everything now." She mocks me. "'I don't want to kill the catatonic girl because I'm depressed.' 'I'm physically incapable of having zombie sex in the screaming room and making the humans watch because I'm depressed.' Is that what you're going to say about everything from now on?"

Am *I* your problem? Is our *marriage* your problem? Should we just dissolve this, all of this, like another teaspoon of salt in the undrinkable water of the world? It's already impure, right? It's like Guy Boy Man says, "Good always comes from bad so by doing bad we increase the good."

"Look," I say. "I'm sorry I'm not the perfect husband. I'm sorry I'm not whatever the hell you want. Barry Graves probably. He's so handsome and sensitive. When I'm done eating Constance, we'll go into the stupid screaming room and I'll give you a stupid five-minute distraction from your own stupid unhappiness."

She shuffles to face me; her expressionless face is disgusted. "You're a real romantic, Buck."

I wrench one of Constance's forelegs back and forth. Bones crack. Everything gives in to strength; to force; to violence: tendons, ligaments, muscles. I tear off Constance's leg. I hold it up to her. "Do you want some?"

She fumes: putrefaction, decay, rancid rot. "No, I don't want some. I can't believe you just asked me if I want some."

"Are you sure?" I keep holding it up to her. "Good kitty."

"What is it, Buck?" she asks, suddenly sincere. "What's the matter? Aren't I enough for you?"

I take a bite and chew. "You're making this into something more than it is. I just wanted to eat cat."

I don't know why she always wants to talk about everything. We never resolve anything. We just keep talking.

"This is an indication," she says, accusing me. She points at me with her arms. "This *says something* about our *relationship*."

"Come on, Chi. You know this happens. It's perfectly natural. It goes on in zombie houses all the time. It probably happens in, I don't know, fifty percent of zombie homes."

"I think that number is a little high."

"Twenty-six-point-nine percent. Whatever. They only come down on you if you eat somebody else's cat."

"I'm not worried about that, Buck. I'm worried about our relationship. Relationships are based on trust and communication."

I don't know anymore. I don't know *what* I know anymore. Before I started feeling so miserable, I never thought Chi might be cheating on me. Now I think she is. All the time. I think I'm the biggest idiot that ever lived. I think she and Barry Graves are meeting in secret whenever they can. They're laughing at me. They're having passionate sex and afterwards they're laughing at me. At how stupid I am. It makes me furious.

"I can't do anything right as far as you're concerned!" I cry. "You're never happy! And it's always my fault! All you do is criticize me! I don't do this; I don't do that. But then, when I make the effort and I try, you're not satisfied with the result because it's not exactly the same as when *you* do it! You show me the right way, like I'm stupid. Like I'm"—I wave the arm around some more—"an infant!"

"It isn't . . . ! I don't mean . . . !"

"You make doctor's appointments for me!" I yell, telepathically. "You practically try to force feed me! I'm not a child, Chi! Stop mothering me!"

"I care about you, Buck! I worry! You haven't been looking after yourself! You quit eating human flesh! You took a shower! With soap! I'm pretty sure you even washed your clothes!"

"I. Never. Washed. My. Clothes."

"What was I supposed to do?"

"I don't know. Maybe you could've given me a little space! Maybe I'm going through some things right now! Maybe I'm trying to work some stuff out!"

"How am I supposed to know that? You never told me that!"

"I think it's pretty obvious!"

"What do you want from me, Buck? Do you want me to sit back and watch you starve to death?"

"Well I'm eating now!" I take another bite of cat. I point at myself with bone. With my mouth full, I say, "What do you want from *me*, Chi? Do you want me to completely give in to you? Do you want me to do *whatever* you want, *whenever* you want? Is that who you thought you were marrying? Some whipped chump who was going to work all day, come home and make supper, and rub your feet while you watch TV? Well I'm sorry, but that's not me! I'm not your plaything! I'm not your slave! I'm not going to let you keep me chained up!"

"That's not what I want!"

"What *do* you want?"

"I just." She sends me silence. She sends me her search for words she can't find and that don't exist. "I don't know," she says, finally, with a sigh. "I want you to talk to me before you eat the cat."

I know Chi is ready to make peace now but it isn't over. It's never over. It's insurmountable. The same things just keep happening. "What good would talking have done? You would've tried to talk me out of it."

"Of course I would!"

"See? That's why I didn't talk to you about it."

Her shoulders fall. "I don't know what's happening here, Buck. I really don't."

I finally swallow. "Nothing is happening here. I'm eating some cat. That's it. I'll replace it. It's not a big deal." With my jagged teeth, I pull and tear the last of the meat from the legs. Chewing, I drop the little bones on the floor with the others.

"It's a big deal to me!"

"Maybe I should make you a doctor's appointment," I say, snidely. "He can put you on anti-depressants. Then it won't bother you." Why am I being like this? Why am I egging her on? Do I *want* her to leave me?

"You blame me for everything!" cries Chi.

"No! You won't accept responsibility for anything!"

"Fine. It's my fault. Are you happy now? It's all my fault." Hurt, she shakes her head and looks away.

"It's not *entirely* your fault. It's *partly* your fault."

"Well, thanks for your generosity." She's still not looking at me. "Since you're being so kind, please, tell me exactly *which* part is my fault?"

"The mothering part."

"Which part is *your* fault?"

"Not expressing my feelings and wishes in an open and honest manner and instead seething with furious resentment that I directed inward when I should've directed it toward you."

"Yeah," she laughs, angrily, turning back to me, nodding. "That sounds like it would've made our lives *a lot* better."

"You want to know what this is?" I lift up what's left of Constance: what's left of her corpse. Limp, she hangs in pieces. Held together by sinew and ligament, tendon and bone, she dangles. "This is an *incensed* comment on how I, willingly, gave up my genetic imperative to sleep with as many females as possible to be with you but you didn't give up your genetic imperative to have children to be with *me*! I never wanted to have a kid in the first place, Chi! You talked me into it!"

"We agreed!"

"No." I drop Constance onto the table. "You *argued*. I gave in."

"I can't believe you, Buck. I really can't."

CHAPTER EIGHTEEN

Everything Human And Afraid

Chi goes nuts when I insist I never wanted Francis Bacon. She loses her mindless mind. She screams at me, soundlessly. Telepathically, she floods me with curses and castigations. She rants that I'm not a real zombie; a real zombie doesn't cry; I'm clean; I think; the only thing I'm destroying is our marriage.

I can't take it. I go into the Screaming Room and close the door. I lean back against it in case Chi tries to push it. The bare bulb in a metal cage flicks on and glows dull yellow.

The plump woman sees me and starts screaming, hoarsely, scrambling backwards into a corner. The catatonic girl wakes, gently, and stares at me with something closer to pity than disgust. Flies swirl around the light like little bits of dark.

I don't know what makes me think of it; what makes me remember: the package of butterflies Fairy_26 gave me; the butterflies I can use to call her. I reach into my pocket and get it. It's such a delicate operation. I don't know if I can do it. I fall to my knees in wordless prayer, to beg for life.

For the first time, the catatonic girl seems interested. I try to wipe a clean spot on the filthy floor. It doesn't work. I can only spread the mess around. Realizing it isn't going to get any better, I set down the package. I open it. As carefully as I can, I withdraw a perfectly flat butterfly. Is it asleep or dormant? I don't know. It's such a beautiful and fragile thing. It reminds me of Fairy_26. It's so peaceful. I search for it and search for it. There's no safe place to set it down. Cautiously, the catatonic girl crawls toward me. When she's within arms' reach, she kneels, wipes her hands on her legs, on her breasts, on her hair, everywhere and anywhere she can think of, trying to get them clean; not immaculate; just clean enough. In a gesture beyond my comprehension, ultimately, she licks them. She does it with her eyes closed and her face scrunched. She licks off blood, excrement, desperate sex, and sick. She licks off everything human and afraid. She gags but doesn't stop. When she thinks she has it, she opens her eyes. Satisfied, she waves them in the foul air, drying them. She rubs them together. Then she holds them open to me and nods. I set the butterfly on her palms. I just stare at it for a minute; its patterns: spots, blotches, streaks, and serrations; its colors: orange, black, yellow, and white.

Why would nature do something like this? Chance? Luck? Why would God? Cruelty? I pick up the other package. I open it. Carefully, I tip and tap it. Dust sprinkles onto the butterfly. Immediately, it begins opening and closing its wings, testing them. Its antennae move around. Staring at the amazing creature, the catatonic girl smiles and says, "Good morning, Painted Lady."

Suddenly the butterfly lifts off the catatonic girl's hand and flutters around the room. I didn't realize it when it happened but now I notice the plump woman has stopped screaming. She's staring at the butterfly, flitting around the room and her eyes, like she must be dreaming.

The catatonic girl waves her hand in front of my face, getting my attention. She gestures toward the door. I understand: open it.

Awkwardly, I get to my feet. I amble to the door. I open it and look back over my shoulder. The catatonic girl is going back to where she was before, physically and mentally. I watch her leave. The plump woman isn't looking at the butterfly anymore. She's seeing something in her mind: a question she knows she'll never answer. I don't know how I know I don't need to look after the butterfly now but I do. It wings its way out of the Screaming Room before I can close the door.

Seeing it, Chi starts yelling at the top of her telepathic lungs. She stumbles away from it, in horror. It terrifies her.

"Kill it!" she yells. "Buck, for God's sakes. This isn't funny. You know I'm scared of butterflies." She drops to her knees and crawls under the table. "Kill it, Buck! Kill it!"

I open the front door. The butterfly flits out into the orange streetlight dark. I watch it for as long as I can.

"All right. It's gone. Thank heavens. Buck? Buck, what are you doing? Close the door! Close it! You're going to let out the rats!"

CHAPTER NINETEEN

We Need To Talk

Five minutes after I let out the butterfly, there's a knock at the door. It's a soft knock, a sacred, scared knock; fairy knuckles on a zombie's door. She's on one side; I'm on the other. Is she thinking and feeling about me the same way I'm feeling and thinking about her? Can fairies be as excited, confused, and scared as zombies?

"Who's that?"

"It's for me," I say, stumbling away from Chi. I trip over a corpse and fall. Clumsily, I get back up. "I forgot to tell you. I'm going out." I take off my jacket and throw it on the floor. "I have to go out. I'm sorry."

"What do you mean? You're going out? You can't go out." She staggers after me. "We need to talk." Chi's evening gown has become her: a thing of stiffness, rigidity, stains, and holes: pieces are missing but not missed; they're just currently, quite possibly forever, unavailable; through no act of will, just happenstance of assembly, the material, or what's left of it, remains whole but it doesn't move in the air she stirs.

"No. You need to talk. And I don't want to listen." I jerk off my tie and whip it at the wall.

"Buck, I don't like this. Who's out there? What's going on? You're getting all dressed up. What are you doing?"

"I don't know what I'm doing, Chi. Stop following me." I yank open the door, step out, and slam it behind me. Then I pull on it, keeping it closed.

Behind me, Fairy_26 hovers a few feet off the ground. "What's going on?" She's wearing skimpy bedtime clothes—a backless white T-shirt and short tight pink boy-shorts—like the butterfly woke her, and she raced right over. "What are you doing?" She says the same things as my wife. She uses the same words. It sounds so different coming from Fairy_26. Will it always be like this? Or will I get sick of her voice like I'm sick of my wife's?

"I don't know," I groan, still holding the door shut. "I don't even know if I'm the one doing it. It might be the albinos in my head. Why am I even talking to you? The pill wore off. You can't understand me."

"I made another one," says Fairy_26. Behind me, she paces in mid-air, flying back and forth, nervously. "It probably won't last as long as the first one and the next one won't last as long as this but I made another one. It's interesting. The formula is a song that sounds great at first but, after a while, you wonder why you ever liked it.

"Anyway. I figured I might as well make another pill. When I felt your butterfly, I took it. I probably should've waited until I was sure it was really important but I didn't think you'd call unless it was really important so I took it. I'm talking a lot, aren't I? I'm scared. I don't know why I'm scared. Why are holding the door closed? Who's pulling on the other side?"

"My wife."

"Yikes." Fairy_26 flies up right behind me, wraps her arms around me, and pulls me straight up into the night. Beneath us, I see the door to my house open. I see Chi step outside. She looks from side to side. She can't find me. She gets smaller and smaller as Fairy_26 takes me higher and higher into the eerie orange night. At a certain point in the sky, in Fairy_26's arms, my wife completely disappears.

CHAPTER TWENTY

One Is Too Many

Inside Fairy_26's tree-branch apartment, I shuffle over to where the structure ends and the sky begins and I look out at Fairyland and all its colours. All the plants here glow soft mint green in the dark. The flowers have closed for the night but the lights are still on inside: red, white, and blue. Fireflies as big as busses drive down invisible streets in the air, carrying supernatural creature passengers on their legs like pollen; their taillights are bright enough to leave tracks on my sightless eyes.

Fairy_26 walks up beside me. She puts a hand on my back and the side of her head against my arm. I don't need to look to see her eyes are closed. If time stopped right now and I could forget my wife and the albinos left me alone, I think I could be happy. That's how ridiculous it is. How many impossible things would have to happen? What's the use in counting? One is too many.

I pull away from Fairy_26. I amble over and flop down on her moss-cushioned sofa. I don't need to see her looking at me. I can feel it. I don't know how it makes me feel. How do I feel? Somebody, teach me. Please. I don't know how to feel.

"What is it, Buck?" asks Fairy_26, lifting her right leg, bending it beneath her, and sitting on it, next to me, on the sofa. She starts pulling bits of garbage from my head.

"I don't know what I'm doing," I confess.

"You're not doing anything," she says, sprinkling something she's taken from me onto the floor.

"Whose happiness is most important?" I ask, turning to her.

"Yours." She says it like it's a silly question. She says it like the answer is obvious. She says it staring at my lips.

"I don't know." I turn away from her. "I have responsibilities. Duties."

"You're a zombie," she admits.

"I don't want to want what I want but I can't help it. I don't want what I have but I have it." I turn toward her again. "You know?"

She smiles sadly. She nods.

I turn away again. "I don't even know how much of this is me." I look at my undead arms: stretched out; reaching out. "I'm not in control of anything. I don't know why it took albinos for me to realize it. I knew it before. I'm not in control of anything. I'm like one of those plants out there"—I gesture at the hole in the wall—"moving with the wind."

"Those plants have roots," she says, comfortingly.
"Yeah," I agree. "But in what?"

CHAPTER TWENTY-ONE

I Know You're Married And You're A Zombie But I Can't Help The Way I Feel

To my right, Fairy_26 kneels, facing me, on the sofa. "Do you want to be with me?" she asks. "Because there are ways, Buck."

I don't know how it started. I think that's the problem. I don't know how it began. If I knew the initial conditions, maybe I could figure out where it's headed, but I showed up in the middle, maybe nearer the end, and I can't understand what's happening; I don't have the information.

"I don't want you to do anything you don't want to do," she assures me. "And I don't want you to do anything you'll regret. I just want you to be happy."

What would make me happy? I love my wife, don't I? I don't want to hurt her, do I? No matter how angry I get with her? No matter how badly she makes me feel? Is it all a memory now? When she could excite me the way Fairy_26 excites me? Is that all gone? If it is, why am I holding onto it? Right now I feel like I'm holding on to something that isn't there anymore. I *say* I honour my commitments. I say I'm contractually obligated to remain faithful my wife until someone bashes out our brains but I *know* infidelity is common among married zombies; I *know* it's typical zombie behaviour. But I don't understand my desires and I'm sick of being mindless. I want there to be a good reason for this feeling. Do I honestly think Fairy_26 could make me happy? If so, for how long?

Is the *need* I *think* I *feel* for her just a chemical reaction to this situation? How involved are the albinos? Ninety percent? Are the albinos pushing me in a certain direction? Are they guiding me away from Chi? Are they leading me to Fairy_26?

"I don't want to do anything the albinos want me to do," I confess.

"What do the albinos want you to do?"

"I don't know."

Fairy_26 puts both hands on the sides of my face and turns me to face her. "If they're in your head and they can make you *feel* whatever they want you to feel and they can make you *think* whatever they want to think, how can you *ever* know you're not doing what the albinos want you to do?"

"I don't know."

CHAPTER TWENTY-TWO

Buck Burger, Where On God's Zombie-Infested Dystopia Have You Been?

Why do I keep going home? Why don't I just leave? Why don't I just pick a direction and go that way until I get somewhere? That's just it. How can I pick a direction when I'm so aimless? And how will I ever know I've gotten somewhere? How long will it take to find out? What if I'm wrong? That's why I go home. It's easy. I don't have to think about it. I just have to dread it.

"Buck Burger, where on God's zombie-infested dystopia have you *been*? I've been standing here with my arms outstretched . . ."

It starts as soon as I open the door. It's a barrage. An assault. Recriminations and accusations fill my brain. I only catch chewed off bits and bloody pieces. " . . . and of all the miserable clean things you've ever done . . ."

Irritated, realizing I'm being mentally shelled from offshore and there's nothing I can do, I throw my keys outside among the skeletons and partly consumed corpses on the front lawn.

"Oh, so *now* you throw your keys, huh?" she says, sarcastically.

She's dressed for war, all in black: black high heels, black leggings, a knee-length, stretchy, black sweater dress. The blood on her dress is drying and pulling the knit in new directions; it bunches the fabric toward it; the material is a zombie, drawn to the wet, warm, sticky red. She almost looks good. Even though she's dead and rotting; unfeeling and thoughtless. She almost looks good, covered in black and blood. Neither her dress nor her leggings have tears or holes; no openings through which I can see her. She's so upset she's letting herself go. Good. I like her when I can't see her. I smash my briefcase against the wall. The briefcase bursts. In the air, papers shoot out like trapped butterflies escaping. The empty briefcase falls to the floor. The papers follow, slower, more gracefully. There's a new hole in the wall.

"*Now* you smash your briefcase against the wall." She says it in the same mocking tone.

I never liked the look of her body, of her skin, even when she was alive. I loved her and I was passionate about her and I'd undress her with an anger, a fury with her, for getting dressed, for keeping her skin from me, for slowing me down, even if it was only a matter of moments but then, after we had sex, I was always upset with myself for being overtaken by the living human animal in me, by giving in to it, by becoming it, and having my fill.

I was always disgusted by the act for which I'd been so hungry and thirsty only minutes earlier and although I never let it show—I was tender and kind—and I pretended I was still enchanted by her physical self and I held her and whispered love words afterwards because I thought it was what she wanted, I would've been happier if she'd just left and returned the next time I wanted her like that. I'd see her get up and walk to the bathroom naked and I'd wonder how I could ever desire that. When I wasn't taking her or having her, I liked her better when she was dressed. When her body was left to my imagination, it was ideal. In my mind, she was someone she could never really be. How could I call it love when I felt this coldly about her body? That was it. It was just her body. Her body wasn't what I loved. I had sex with her body and that's what was so frustrating about it. She wasn't, and no one could ever be, as wonderful in the flesh as she was in my mind. With so many plans, dreams, and exciting ideas, with a different take on everything, including everything about me, she was my best friend. The universe wasn't enough for us to discuss. We had to invent new ones. Sometimes it seemed we only ever did things apart so we'd have something to dissect, analyze, and laugh about later. Now I just let her vent. She rants and rails. I haven't even closed the door; I've just opened it, walked inside the entryway, and let her furious words splash over me like so much gushing life becoming death. I remember when I used to care, when I'd listen, when I'd say her name every time she paused. "Chi," I'd say;

"Chi, please." Now I just let her go. She's one of those dolls with a string that's been pulled. You can try to reason with it but it's just going to keep talking until it's said everything it has to say. You might as well just wait. I walk into the non-living room. On the sofa, there's an open-mouthed flesh-covered male head from which the brains have been eaten. Looks like Chi had a snack before I got home. Probably thought she needed her strength. I roll the head off onto the floor. I collapse on the spot where the brainless male head had been.

"Do you have anything you want to tell me?" she asks, glaring at me with her sightless white eyes.

I don't say, "I have a lot of things I want to tell you." I don't say, "I have so many things I want to tell you I don't know where to start so I don't start anywhere." Instead I say, calmly, "I don't think so."

"You don't think so or you know you don't?"

"Just get it over with, Chi, okay? I'm tired."

"You're tired?" Chi is incredulous. "You're tired? Really? Me too. I got up early to make lunch for Francis Bacon. When he woke, I had a long talk with him about how you accidentally let out Constance, his cat, and now she's missing. He's going to have a great day at school, isn't he? Get lots of learning done, I'm sure. Yeah, so, I told your unwanted son that you were really upset because it's your stupid fault Constance is gone. I assured him the only reason you, his loving father, were unable to be here to help comfort him during this difficult time is because you're out looking for Constance. In fact, you didn't come home at all last night. You were so sorry for what you'd done, you spent all night searching."

"Oh," I say. "That."

"Yeah. That."

"I'm sorry, Chi. I'm going through some things."

"Depression," says Chi. "I wish I'd never made that doctor's appointment for you. I wonder what sort of excuse you'd dream up for this if the doctor hadn't given you an excuse."

"I have a prescription," I remind her.

"Are you taking your pills as prescribed?"

"No," I admit. "But I got the prescription filled. I thought that was pretty good. I mean, I didn't even feel like doing that."

"Great, Buck. Congratulations. It sounds like you're really on the road to recovery. No. Actually, it sounds like you *were* on the road to recovery but then you stopped and you got hit by a car." In our minds, in disgust, she shakes her head. "A big car. Going very quickly."

"Is that it?" Clumsily, I start trying to get up from the sofa.

"No, Buck. That's not it."

I fall back down into the sofa's soft cushions. The cushions are covered by beige fabric covered with blood that's dried red-brown and started to break into little flakes.

"What else?"

"Deepah called," says Chi. "Barry says you got promoted. Did you get promoted, Buck?"

"Yes," I admit. "But it's not that bad." I assure her. "Not all our friends will start treating us like pariahs."

"Why'd you get promoted, Buck?" she whines.

"I don't know. I didn't want to get promoted."

"You're an executive, Buck! An executive!"

"I'm sorry, Chi. I never wanted this to happen. I thought I was keeping my head down."

"Do you have stock options? Be honest with me! Do you have stock options?"

"Yes," I sigh.

"What else?" she demands.

I don't answer right away. I go through the list in my mind, picking a few things that don't seem that bad. "A car and driver. Access to the company jet." I pretend I'm still trying to remember. "I think that's it."

"A raise? Are you getting a raise, too?"

"Wait. No, yeah. They might have said something about a raise," I admit, embarrassed.

"Buck Burger, don't tell me you have an expense account!" she warns, pointing at me in our minds. "Don't tell me you have an expense account now! Don't do it!"

"I'm sorry!" I cry. "I'm sure it'll be audited! I won't be able to get away with much!"

"Did they tell you it was going to be audited?"

"Not directly."

"I can't believe this!" She turns, staggers away a few steps, and turns back. "You're ruining our non-life! What are we going to do with all that money? Do you know how hard it's been to keep this place even mildly squalid with the two incomes we already had?"

"We'll find a way, Chi," I reassure. "We'll make it work."

If she were alive, she'd be crying now. She'd be sobbing. As it is though, she just stares at me through disgusting white eyes. "What am I supposed to tell my friends, Buck? Huh? What am I supposed to tell my friends?"

"It's not my fault!" I yell.

"Because you're depressed?"

"Yeah! Because I'm depressed!" I gesture at my head, stiffly. "It's neuro-chemical." I think about the albinos in my mind and, still rigidly pointing at my brain, I insist, "There are forces at work beyond my control!"

"Can you do anything now, Buck? Can you do whatever you want? Do you live in a world free of consequences because you're depressed?"

"I don't know about free of consequences, Chi, but it's pretty free of happiness, okay?"

"And I'm sure this argument isn't helping anything. Right? I'm contributing to your unhappiness? Your depression?" Furious, Chi ambles off, into our bedroom.

Trying and failing to get up from the sofa, I call after her: "Look. I'm sure the other executives have this same problem. I'll ask them about it, okay? And I know what you're saying. You're right. We probably won't keep all the friends we already have because they won't want to be around nicer broken things in more elegant blood-splattered, feces- and sick-covered rooms and they probably won't want to eat glamorous people and that's sad but maybe we'll make new friends. Executive friends. They must socialize, right?"

"You'll probably want me to buy a new dress," Chi calls from the bedroom. "An expensive one."

"You can tear it and stain it as soon as you get it just like you do with the new dresses you get now." I can't get up from this stupid sofa! My gnarled senseless grey hands sink deep into the foam cushions! My stiff legs won't bend far enough for me to roll forward up onto them!

After a long pause from Chi, she says, "You think I *ever* buy new dresses?"

Now I pause for a while. "Don't you?"

"Of course not! God, Buck! I take them from the women I kill and eat in the street!"

"I'm sorry! Okay? I just assumed!"

"Sometimes it feels we don't know each other at all!"

I don't say, "I wish I knew the feeling." Instead I say, "I'm sorry, Chi! Jeez! I wasn't implying anything!"

She stumbles out of the bedroom, carrying a suitcase full of soiled clothes and fresh human body-parts. "I'm going to stay with Deepah and Barry."

"That's right," I say, fighting to stand up, for, I don't know, something I don't understand, myself. "Run off to your boyfriend, Barry."

"He's not my boyfriend, Buck," she snorts. "He's my best friend's husband. Nothing has, or will, ever happen between Barry and me."

"What about Francis Bacon?" I ask, stopping my struggle. "Huh? What about your son?"

"He should be home from school soon," she says, stomping on, cracking, and breaking bones on her way to the front door. Reaching the front door, she opens it. "Tell him I'm at Deepah and Barry's, if he needs me." Before she leaves, she turns and looks at me. "If he needs you, tell him you're depressed!" She slams the door behind her.

CHAPTER TWENTY-THREE

Everything Seems To Happen Now

Time seems to stop, waiting for Francis Bacon to get home from school. I don't know what time does. I don't know how it works. Everything seems to happen now. It rushes in from both sides. It smothers me. I don't know what to tell Francis Bacon. Not the truth. I can't tell him the truth. That's probably the thing that's surprised me most about being a father: how rarely I tell my son the truth. Everything is a lie aimed at turning him into something I'm not. I'm not sure the lies work because they didn't for me but the truth is so terrible. How could I ever tell anyone the truth? I spend most of my time trying not to admit it to myself.

Francis Bacon is a good-looking young man. I don't think he has a girlfriend but I don't know. I don't think he has a boyfriend, either, but I don't know. If he has a group of friends at school, that's where he keeps them.

He doesn't get many phone calls here. He doesn't go out often. He keeps to himself, even in the family. He's pleasant and polite. Sure, he and I get into fights. He doesn't have his music loud enough. He doesn't drink or smoke enough. We never walk in on him having sex with some girl. It's regular family stuff. "Francis Bacon, are the cops ever going to come looking for you?" You know. That sort of thing.

Francis Bacon, who are you?

I have such mixed feelings about him. I love him. I mean, I think I love him. I don't know. I'm not sure what love is and it seems like there are so many different kinds and all the different kinds get swirled up with frustration, impatience, worry, and resentment.

Francis Bacon took his mother from me. When Francis Bacon was born, Chi became a different person. She tried not to. She tried to keep everything the same but it was impossible and we both knew it. I knew it before she did. I pouted. I walked around feeling sorry for myself. For a while, she tried to cheer me up. When she'd put Francis Bacon down for the night, she'd get dressed in torn lingerie and holey stockings and broken high heels and beckon me into the locked and padded room where we keep the living people we eat. Sometimes we'd make love in front of our groceries, turned on by their terror. Sometimes, as foreplay, we'd arouse each other by killing a member of the same sex. As we fed, tearing off and chewing chunks of human flesh, while blood spurted on and spilled down our faces and naked bodies, we'd have telepathic table-talk, discussing how the screaming faces of our food, contorted in pain, were like sex faces, and how it was strange that the faces of making life were the same as the faces of facing death. Having sex in the warm, sticky, salty wet, we agreed red was a wonderful colour choice. But after a while, Chi got tired of trying to cheer me up. She started telling me to grow up. I don't know if I did or not. I think I just shut up. And part of me shut down. Has that part been awoken by Fairy_26?

I've been trying not to think of her. But I do. I think of her so often and in so many different ways. She's infected me with health. She's poisoned me with the memory of well-being. She's killing me to life. I think about her hair: how green it is; how soft it looks, and how shiny; I imagine holding it, not in my tree-root-excuse for hands, but in my old alive hands; I imagine her locks spilling between my fingers. I think about her eyes: they're so blue, the colour of cold and death, but so warm and alive; between blinks, they go from concern to smile, from fear to hope, from loss to lust. I see myself in them, my reflection, and I don't look as bad as I feel. I imagine seeing myself through them and I look better. I don't imagine her doing the things I used to imagine women doing before I became a zombie. I don't imagine her naked. I don't imagine her doing anything sexual. Even though she can hover. I imagine her clipping her fingernails; pushing back her cuticles. I imagine her brushing her teeth; flossing. I imagine her doing her makeup; her hair. I imagine her getting ready for me.

Then, in my mind, I shake my head, trying to get rid of these thoughts, fears, hopes; I don't know what they are. I just know they're too much for me. Too much to dream; too dangerous to consider. I love my wife. I say it over and over to myself. It's my mantra; a prayer. There's the danger: the more I say it, the less it means. It's becoming letters and sounds: representing nothing. I hold onto it because it's in my hands. It's pulling me somewhere. Toward something, away from something, or both? Should I find out or let go?

Francis Bacon, have you done this to me? Did you take your mother from me? Did she leave me for you? If this is a competition, you win. She wanted you before she ever met me but if we're trying to share her, I'm not getting enough. You can't be getting enough of her, either. She's not getting enough of herself. She's just like us. Doomed. She doesn't know what she wants but she keeps trying to get it. What are we going to do?

Maybe Francis Bacon won't come home; the thought shines a light into my dark mind. Maybe, for some secret teenage reason, he has to leave. Maybe he's in love with someone. Maybe he's running away with her. Or him. I don't care. Just don't come back. Just go and forget us. I can't say your mother and I will be fine. I can't say you'll be fine. We won't. You won't. But maybe, just maybe, if only for one day, you'll be more alive than anyone has ever been, with suitcases in the backseat, one hand on the steering wheel, and one arm around that special someone. Turn up the music; drive fast; laugh for no reason or because you're scared; don't know where you're going; never get there; and may you never get sick of trying. I wish you could. I wish you would. You'll be home any time now.

I'm afraid of the door. It could open any second. Will it be a good one? The second it opens could close everything around us. Will it protect us or kill us? I could leave before Francis Bacon comes home. I could open the door myself and of possibility in myself. It'd change everything. I could open the door and walk out and never come back. I could do anything. I think that's the most difficult thing to remember or maybe just the most difficult thing to comprehend. I could do anything.

I roll off the sofa, onto the floor. I end up face to face with the male head, the brains from which Chi ate, the mouth of which is open in horror. It's like looking in the mirror.

After a minute of rolling around and failed attempts, I manage to get up. I amble to the locked and padded room in which we keep the living people we eat. After fumbling with the mechanisms, I get the door open. Hanging from the ceiling, the solitary bulb flickers on, stirring the flies, drawing them off the floor and walls, away from the bodily fluids, toward the light, which they buzz around; they're so scared to land on it; it gets so hellishly hot. There's only one person left, alive, in the padded room. Naked, the catatonic girl who helped me wake the butterfly sits in a corner, holding her knees to her chest. I stagger out of the room, leaving the door open behind me.

Unafraid it's a trap, or recognizing she doesn't have much to lose, the catatonic girl gets up and follows me a few moments later. I've already trudged to the front door, the door I'm afraid of someone else opening; I've opened it myself. The mid-afternoon sun drips in, filtered through heavy blue rain clouds. The fresh air is like a shower with soap in all this house's rot and corruption. Bored flies lazily buzz out, away from all the sick they can eat, into the cold clean world we, the zombies, keep trying to warm with random fires and to prove we've visited by wrecking everything we can't find.

I'm standing next to the open door. Unintentionally, my outstretched arms block the catatonic girl's path to survival; I don't even notice until she, bravely, ducks underneath them and moves past me, beyond me, somewhere I can never go. She hurries to the street. Then she stops. With her back to me, she stands there for a second, waiting. Maybe she's waiting to see if this is a game, if she's going to hear me groan and stumble toward her, or if, even worse, she's going to feel my claw hands on her naked shoulders. Maybe she's thinking I just want a picnic on the front lawn. Then, mustering the courage, or realizing the truth, she turns back. I'm still standing in the entryway. I'm just watching.

"Why?" she says.

I can't answer. I don't speak her language. Even if I did, I'm not sure I could explain. I'm not sure I understand it myself. I just don't want to eat her. I don't want to eat anyone ever again. I didn't want to eat the cat. I was just so angry. Not at Chi. At the world. Zombies, supernatural creatures. I thought I was doing Constance a favour. It was quick and painless. You can't say that about life.

"Well, thank you," says the catatonic girl.

I can't do either but I wonder, if I could, whether I'd laugh or cry. I want to do something nice, wonderful, for someone, everyone, everything, and I tried to do it for this catatonic girl but at the same time, I'm the one who kept her in a locked and padded room, suffering with knowledge: at any moment, she could be eaten.

"You're welcome," I think.

I watch her turn and go. She walks for a while. Then she starts running. She runs so quickly. I hear her bare feet smacking the concrete. The sound echoes off the houses and rings sharply in my undead ears. I watch her until she turns into Francis Bacon, running home from school, at the point in the distance where everything becomes more confused and true. I go back inside and close the door.

A few minutes later, Francis Bacon rushes in. He's stopped being my son. He's a force. He's words and energy. "Did you find Constance?" he asks, breathless. "Did she come back? It was so cold last night. You don't think she froze to death, do you?"

I don't know what to say. All the lies seem true and the truth seems like a lie.

"Dad?"

Why did I stay here for this?

"What's wrong, Dad?"

I want to kill him. I want to kill Francis Bacon, to protect him: from me; the truth. I want to give him a chance to avoid my fate: to know how much at fault you are. I don't want him to know, like I know, when I'm honest with myself, undead people, like me, are the problem and must be stopped but it's so much easier to become me than to stop me because to stop me you must stop yourself. It's easier not to think. It's easier to be mindless. And everyone else is anyway.

"Dad? You're scaring me. Just tell me what's going on. I can handle it, whatever it is. We'll get through it together. Right? That's what you always say."

"Constance is dead."

Francis Bacon drops his backpack. When he was running home, he had it slung over one shoulder. When he got inside, he let it slip to his hand, and he held it by one strap. Now it's on the floor. Dropping his backpack is Francis Bacon's physical acknowledgment of a horrible truth. Perhaps it'd be more meaningful if the backpack contained a few key books, the titles of which would reflect his feelings right now, but I don't know what books he has in his backpack. It's closed. Zippered shut. Like fate.

Here's a mindless thought: maybe the books are trying, in some imperceptible way, like we are, to escape.

"What happened?"

Francis Bacon asks that and I don't know if he means what happened to Constance, what happened to himself just then, what happened to me, what happened to the world, what ever happened, if anything, or what. I want to say I don't know because I feel like it's truest but I don't. Instead I tell the truth, which seems far less true.

"I ate her."

"What?"

"I ate Cónstance, last night, when you were sleeping."

"Mom?" He calls out, "Mom?"

"Your mother is at the Graves'. I think she'll be staying with them for a while."

Realizing he isn't going to get any help from his mother, at least not immediately, Francis Bacon turns his attention back to me.

"I'm a zombie." I tell Francis Bacon, my son, half me, half my wife, the union and division of our love: "I'm a zombie."

He frowns at me.

I explain: "I'm bad, okay? I know you thought I was good but you were wrong. I'm a zombie. There's no such thing as a good zombie. Don't shake your head. Listen. I don't want you to learn from my example anymore. I'm mindless. I do things because I'm supposed to, not because I want to, not because I understand all the factors involved, including my own motivations, predispositions, and emotional state. I do things because I'm supposed to. The albinos want me to. They probably want me to do this. There's no escape. Get away from me, Francis Bacon. Find a few likeminded people, arm yourselves, barricade yourselves in a secure location with plenty of food, potable water, and condoms, and kill every damn zombie trying to eat or infect you. Bash out their brains; chop up their bodies; light the pieces on fire. When you realize no help is coming, kill yourselves. I wish I had the courage to do what I know is right. Maybe you will."

Francis Bacon runs to his bedroom and slams the door.

"While you're packing," I call to him, "keep in mind, winter is coming. You don't need to be fashionable. You need to be warm and dry. Layers. Think layers. Pack light. You can loot most of what you need. Hit a sporting goods store, as soon as possible. You want a good winter coat, a good sleeping bag, a few pairs of long underwear. You'll need waterproof pouches for matches, ammunition, and things like that. You're going to be starting fires to cook meals and purifying water to drink, so steal accordingly. Be on the lookout for Kevlar, chainmail, and the mesh suits scuba-divers use to swim with sharks.

"Find yourself a staff: a good wooden stick; and keep it with you always. You'll probably be tempted to go with a metal rod, considering all the zombie skulls you'll be smashing with it, but you don't want something that hastens frostbite in the winter and you're going to be carrying it around a lot so you want something light. When you carry it around for a few years, you might be tempted to trade it in for a plastic model. Don't. Sure, you can sharpen the end of a nice light plastic pole and use the pointed end to pierce zombie skulls but you can and should do that with your wooden staff, too.

"Trust me. Your wooden staff will serve you far better when you're locked in close combat with overwhelming numbers of zombies; you want something with a little heft when you panic and you start swinging wildly. I'm not going to tell you not to panic because you will, and, considering what you're up against, should. Just do as well as you can. If you're lucky, you'll die of natural causes before you know it. If you're unlucky, you'll suffer an agonizing death at the tearing hands and chewing mouths of hungry zombies. If you're miserably unfortunate, they'll infect you, turning you into one of them and you'll be like me. You don't want to be like me. I should know. I'm exactly like me and I don't like it at all. I'm going now! Good luck! And don't forget to get a great staff!"

CHAPTER TWENTY-FOUR

The Destruction Starts Again Tomorrow

I'm back at Fairy_26's tree-branch apartment. A housefly darts past the open wall. I see a couple of creatures I don't recognize behind the controls; behind the compound eyes. All the passengers—the trolls, elves, and dwarves—are in seats in the fly's body. The eyes and body must lose their transparency and gain an opaqueness when they pass into the real world. I lose sight of the housefly in the sun; it's setting, brightly yellow, and pouring golden light over all Fairyland's vibrant green and strong brown. The flower shops—the shops inside flowers—and the mushroom stores—the stores inside mushrooms—are doing a bustling business as most of the day draws to a close with the dawn of evening. Waiting for Fairy_26 to get changed out of her work clothes, I wonder where the housefly is taking its passengers. To work probably. To clean up after the zombie mess. The destruction starts again tomorrow.

"Buck?" calls Fairy_26, from her bedroom. "I'm feeling a little vulnerable right now. When I started getting dressed, I was completely confident but now I'm terrified. I thought I knew what I was doing. Wait. That's not what I meant to say. I know what I'm doing. I just don't know how you're going to take it. I thought you were going to be happy but now I don't know. I don't want to make a fool of myself."

I groan. It's all I can do. Fairy_26 made another pill, using the formula provided by the albinos, but it didn't work; nothing I say makes sense to her; everything I say still sounds like zombie moans.

"Okay," calls Fairy_26. "I'm going to come out but if you don't like it, just tell me. All right, yeah, I know. You can't tell me. That was stupid. Sorry. I don't know. If you don't like it, groan twice. How about that? I can always get changed again and we can pretend this never happened."

Timidly, and blushing pink, Fairy_26 walks out of her bedroom. Her perfect figure is hidden only by a green baby-doll. It's so lustrous it looks almost liquid. Her feet are covered by sparkly blue high heels. The baby-doll matches her green hair, which is done up in curls, hanging, in suspense, around her head and just above her shoulders. Her blue shoes match her wide starry eyes, which are surrounded, waiting to learn their fate, by white eyeliner and smoky black shadow. Nervous, her wings are pressed together, tightly, behind her back. She stands just outside her bedroom door, leaning against the wall—the warm wood inside her tree-branch apartment—with her elegant hands poised above her shapely bare thighs, and with her fingertips touching them. Her shoulders are raised in embarrassment, waiting to hear what I think.

I can't remember if I'm supposed to groan twice if I like it or if I'm supposed to groan twice if I don't like it. It was twice, right? I can't remember what feeling alive feels like but this feels like so much. It feels wonderful. I want to run to her or, at least, stagger and stumble with my arms outstretched. I want to kiss her lips, neck, and shoulders or, at least, not bite hunks of flesh from them. I want to be inside her without infecting her. I want to fly to her but I don't have wings. I don't even trust myself to stand. I just sit. I wait and hope. To feel her warm against my cold; her soft against my hard.

"I forgot something." Fairy_26 disappears back inside her room and emerges, a moment later, with a silver-grey rope and a muzzle. "It's not that I don't trust you. I do." She walks toward me; her baby-doll moves in the breeze she creates; it slips between her legs and presses against the fronts of her thighs and against her breasts; it ripples out everywhere she isn't. "It's just. I heard, sometimes, when what I hope will happen between the two of us happens, people like you lose control and bite. I'm not scared of that but I know you and I know you would be so I got this." She holds up the muzzle and moves close. Burying one of her knees, alive, in the sofa's soft moss cushion she puts it over my undead head. "I got it from a friend. She's more interesting than I thought." The muzzle consists of thin stainless steel bars that bend; they arc over the tops of my ears and around the back of my head; they curve over my nose and under my chin; away from my cold lips, they spread and converge; there's no opening big enough through which to fit even my gross blue-green tongue. When she's done muzzling me, she uses the silver-grey rope to bind my outstretched wrists. "You're very strong, too. You could hurt me, or worse, if you grabbed onto me, and as much as I like the idea of you grabbing onto me"—she smiles— "I know you wouldn't want to take that chance so I got this rope." When she's done securing my hands, she steps back and admires her handiwork. "I think you're safe."

She does things like that. She muzzles and binds me and says, "I think you're safe." Doesn't she mean she's safe? It's adorable.

She clasps her hands in front of herself and suddenly gets shy again. "I've spent a lot of time thinking about how to turn you on. I mean, I know you're turned on. I can tell."

She giggles. "And I'm glad. Believe me. I'm very, very glad. But I've spent a lot of time thinking about how to turn you on so, so much, you can almost feel again. I know you can't, ever, really, feel again but I like you so much, I spent time thinking about how to try. I thought I could clean my apartment in front of you."

The thought almost makes me cry out in emotional pain, in tortured mental anguish; I could never imagine anything so beautiful.

"After that I thought maybe I could give you a nice long bath and get you good and clean."

It's strange how close sex is to suffering. I'm suffering more than ever, thinking of feeling better than ever.

"But then I thought, no. I just want to do it with him. As soon as possible."

Before I know it, it's happening: everything I wanted, and fought, uselessly, not to want. On top of me, with her head between my bound arms, her big blue eyes get bigger than ever; in their black and white makeup frames, they're so brilliantly bright. Her soft shiny green curls bounce like they want to uncurl, but can't. She doesn't take off her baby-doll. I don't know why but I'm glad. The glimpses of her are better than the whole truth could ever be. It reminds me of my wife.

Before we became zombies—before we got married—Chi and I walked from city to city, looking for other living humans with whom we could band. There were quite a few but they were all like we were: desperate to survive; unscrupulously intent on eating, sleeping, and feeling as safe as possible. You couldn't trust any of them. Chi and I would hole up in some abandoned house, eat canned food in the dark, cut strategic holes, and have sex with our clothes on. We had to. If a group of zombies stumbles onto your position, you don't want to be caught with your pants down. Chi was a feral cat back then. Her nails;

her teeth. She hurt me as much as she made me feel better. She was skinny with hunger and taut from cracking zombie skulls. She'd grab me and make me forget about zombies for a while; first, I had to survive her. She hurt me, physically, in ways I didn't mind remembering.

It was so dark at night. There were no candles; no campfires. If you were lucky—and you never were— you found electricity but you were too scared to use it. Zombies are just as attracted to the light as we are. We couldn't turn on anything but each other. Every sound we heard was a threat. Every noise we made was dangerous. We learned how to be quiet. We didn't moan. We didn't call on God and Jesus. We didn't affirm our actions with yeses, oh yeses. We didn't swear out loud. If it was windy or we were near the ocean, we'd let our bodies collide and clap, and maybe, afterwards, allow ourselves a contented sigh.

Chi was smart. I would've followed her anywhere. I did. I followed her right here. Here, where I am now, with a gorgeous green-haired fairy using her fluttering wings to lift herself up on me, and to die, falling down on me, is all because of Chi. We were in whatever city we were in—they all look the same in the evening, when the zombies have torn down everything they can and burnt everything they can and all that's left is broken and smoking—and Chi had been there before. She knew I loved her. I'd told her. I'd told her even before I meant it but then, not long after, I started meaning it. She loved me, too. I'd like to express some doubt about it but, in whatever conscience I ever had and have left now, I can't. She loved me, too.

That's why I still can't understand what she did.

Afterwards, she said she didn't know. She insisted she didn't know. She swore. I didn't believe her then. I still don't. You can be sure she knew. I am.

I forgave her. I forgive her. Forgiveness never stops.

"Do you feel as good as I do?" whimpers Fairy_26.

I groan.

She led me straight into a trap. I don't know if it's because she was tired, of running, trying, fighting, struggling for everything, with everything, against everything. If she was, I couldn't blame her. I was tired. I just wasn't ready to give up. I guess I'm still not. If I was, I could be happy being a zombie but I can't. I can't be happy.

She was a little ways ahead of me. I don't know why I was lagging behind. I can't remember. If I'd been doing something important, I'd remember but I must not have been because I can't. She climbed a chain-link fence. On the other side, a few moments later, zombies staggered, ambled, and stumbled toward her from all directions. She screamed. It was a real scream. It's only natural to scream when you're surrounded by the undead even if you know they're there and they're going to eat you or infect you and she did. She screamed and screamed.

"Oh God! Oh God!"

I don't know when I decided. They say we choose what we do and we have to live with the consequences. Well, I don't remember having the time to consider my options, their pros and cons, taking into account my genetics, upbringing, and current brain chemistry, and how those factors were affecting my perception of my options and their up- and down-sides. And I don't have to live with the consequences of this so-called choice, this ostensible decision, this result I brought about, purportedly, of my own free, quote unquote, will. I have to un-live with it. As a zombie. You know. One of the undead.

Or else it had to be. It was determined: preordained; fate; albinos were behind it.

"Isn't this wonderful?" cries Fairy_26.

I moan.

I don't remember when I started running. I only remember realizing I was. I wasn't running away: that's what I would've done if I'd been conscious of what I was doing. I was running toward her. I was running toward Chi. I'd found a revolver and two shells. Like an idiot, I'd set down my reliable wooden staff, forsaking it for the glamourous killing extension afforded by the revolver. I had it drawn. I wasn't pointing it at the zombies. I was running. I wasn't going to waste either of my two shots by firing in fear and fury. I was going to get close enough. Then I was going to blast out the brains of two of them. There were more than two, though. There were so many more than two. I was running to certain death. Or worse. To becoming a zombie. I was running to Chi.

Throwing back her head, Fairy_26 screams, "You feel so good, Buck!"

ZVFFA

Do I?

I didn't have wings but I flew over that fence. I grabbed one of the zombies clutching Chi, biting her, infecting her and, with Chi's blood spray misting my face, I wheeled the zombie around, stuck the revolver's muzzle right against his cheek, and squeezed the trigger. There was the sound and the zombie's head jerked back. But then the zombie's head rolled back down. With Chi's life-force smeared over its lips, cheeks, and chin, the zombie looked at me, blankly, still undead. I shot again. The zombie's head snapped back again. He looked at me again. I started beating his skull with the butt end of the revolver. Then another zombie grabbed me from behind. I felt its teeth sinking into my thick skin so easily.

"I'm just about! I'm almost!"

"Thank you," laughed Barry Graves, telepathically. He was the zombie that bit Chi, infecting her. He was the zombie I spun around and shot in the face. Twice. "Now I'm going to get a ton of ass. And you should've seen yourself," laughed Barry Graves, telepathically. I aimed right at the top of his head. Even as a zombie, I remember thinking, "This guy must have no brain whatsoever."

Undead now, Chi walked up to me. "I'm sorry, Buck," she said, telepathically. "I didn't know."

I knew she was lying. I saw where we were: City Hall. Wherever you go, it doesn't matter; whatever city you're in, City Hall is pretty much Zombie Central. It didn't matter. I knew when I was running to her.

I didn't care. That's how dumb I was. That's how dumb love made me. Diminished capacity? What about none whatsoever? "Look at it this way, Buck," said Chi, from her mind to mine, smiling slyly but not slyly enough to hide it. "We can be together forever now."

When I was running to Chi, carrying that stupid revolver with only two stupid bullets into a swarm of undead monsters, I remember yelling and yelling.

"I'm coming! I'm coming!"

The whole time I have sex with Fairy_26, I fantasize about my wife.

CHAPTER TWENTY-FIVE

We Need, or Think We Do

Away from Fairyland, back in the real world, I stumble around, not knowing what to do. I want to be with Fairy_26. I want to call her. Right now. With butterflies. I want to see her. I want to hear her. I want to be happy but I'm scared of getting what I want because I might be wrong and I don't want to hurt Chi. As little as we get along and as much as we fight, the thought of hurting Chi makes me miserable. How can the thought of doing what it takes to be happy make me miserable? I join a group of zombies going into a mall. I leave the ones who are actually just going into the outside of the mall, over and over, non-thinking that's a way to enter. I go with the ones smashing through the glass doors. We're inside now, past the sparkling shards, shuffling on the, supernaturally, shiny floors, ambling past the, supernaturally, unbroken windows through which we, if we were looking, could see, supernaturally, well-organized and well-stocked shelves. Living people scream, drop the few things they've managed to stuff into reusable cloth shopping bags, and run in orderly chaos. Desperation gets most of the living. They leave the safety of the night for the danger of the day. They need or think they do. The living always approach malls, warily. They can't see any zombies. There aren't any zombies around. Sometimes only one living person is foolish enough to risk it. He or she dashes inside as soon as the doors open and he or she darts around, quickly abandoning his or her plans. There are bargains. Specials. What began as a trip to acquire lightweight well-built essentials and, maybe, a few exotic items to trade, quickly becomes a crazed attempt to get everything this person has ever wanted, no matter what the costs: in terms of needing to move farther from escape routes, being loaded down by the unnecessary, and having no weapon in hand. When I used to, regularly, eat people in malls, I remembering cornering a pretty young blonde. She was filthy: her dress, legs, face, hair. She was holding a bottle of shampoo. Can you imagine? Shampoo! I remember, thoughtlessly, thinking, you don't need shampoo! You need a weapon! Ideally, a good wooden staff! I grabbed a handful of her hair and lifted her, kicking, off the ground. As she held onto my forearm with both hands over her head, I looked at her, incuriously, like she was a familiar toy and I was a bored child. Then I brought her closer and bit off her lower lip. Her screams; her eyes. Her flesh pulled away from her; it slipped into me. It was sexual. Every time we eat or infect someone, it's sexual. It's how we spread, the undead, our strain. I realize now it was the albinos, working through us when we outlawed abortions, when we outlawed birth control, and when we started baby farms.

We grow our own food now. Since abortions occur naturally and abortions have been outlawed, we force a certain high number of volunteers—young men and women—to breed for us. We select them from maturity section: school. In exchange for the volunteers' services, we don't eat or infect them. At least not right away. We make sure the girls take care of themselves when they're pregnant. We make sure they come to term. When they have their baby or, preferably, babies and come to terms with it, or them, being taken away and moved to maturity section where the young are schooled in routine, monotony, and destruction, the girl who recently gave birth is introduced to new males from whom she can take her pick or is happily reunited with an old favourite! Everyone is happy! Lately, with the help of modern fertility medications, our breeders have been having up to eight babies at once! If, despite our best efforts, a girl has a naturally occurring abortion, she's deemed a murderer and eaten.

With albinos guiding us, and supernatural creatures rebuilding everything we wreck, cleaning everything we despoil, we, the zombies, grow in the numbers every day. We spread to new areas all the time. It won't be long until the world is ours. Sometimes it seems like it already is. Sometimes it seems like it always was.

Now, as I amble through the mall, watching zombies slowly, awkwardly, pursuing their screaming, panicking prey who empty their eco-friendly shopping bags, throwing their biodegradable products at us, uselessly, I wonder if there's a grand scheme; a master plan; I wonder if this is leading somewhere, anywhere, or if the albinos are just seeing how far things will go before the balance is upset between zombie and supernatural.

I'm looking for a way out.

I feel like I'm falling. Whenever I'm not with Fairy_26, I feel like I'm falling. I'm plummeting to certain doom. When I'm with Fairy_26, I feel like I'm flying. She's carrying me through the sky. I'm safe. I'm better than safe: I'm happy, excited, eager to learn what will happen next. With the warm wind in my face, with the bright flowers beneath me, in her hands, in her eyes, I'm alive. I don't know when I decided this, if I decided this, or if or when the albinos informed me this is what's meant to happen or why. I'm leaving Chi. I'm not taking the anti-depressants. I'm not going to marriage counselling. I don't want to explain why I'm so angry: Chi is the reason I'm a zombie. Trap or no trap, I'd be alive right now if it weren't for Chi, if it weren't for my love for her. My love for her was my downfall. Will my feelings for Fairy_26 end any better? I doubt it but for some irrational reason, I really want to find out or, rather, I want to experience all the good parts before, and or in between, any difficulties we run into, laughing, holding hands.

ZVFFA

I wonder if Fairy_26 will have me. I wonder if I'm more than an exotic diversion for her. Am I just a source of information to help Guy Boy Man? Does she really like me? As crazy as it sounds, seems, and would have to be, I think she does. I actually think she likes me. Either there's something wrong with her or I'm not so bad. If it weren't today, if it were any other day, and I hadn't just worn a muzzle, had my wrists bound, and had sex with a green-haired pharmacist fairy, I'd think she was dangerously maladjusted.

But on this turn toward the sun, I think maybe I'm on the good side of bad.

I have to tell Chi and I can't just call her. I'm not sure I owe it to her to tell her in zombie I'm leaving her but my new, better view of myself requires me to tell her in zombie.

I find my way out. Behind me, the zombies feast on the warm bodies of all those foolish enough to risk going inside the mall. Maybe a few managed to sneak away if they had a plan, stuck to it, and fought off temptation. It's the only way to survive. I was tempted away from my reliable wooden staff by a stupid revolver for which I only had two stupid bullets. I blame albinos but it could've been stupidity just as easily, perhaps more easily. Everybody makes mistakes but when you're trying to stay alive in a zombie-infested dystopia, you can't afford them. It's why the wild ones, typically, don't last long.

I exit the mall through a service door, stumbling out behind the backs of the stores where supernatural creatures make their deliveries. I'm among the dumpsters with the day's garbage where I probably belong. I spot a group of teenagers crouched around big duffel bags. They're examining items they managed to grab before zombies could grab them. Their eyes are wide with excitement, having survived their close-call and having been successful in their dangerous venture. Their chests are rising and falling, quickly: an effect of their exertion and their adrenalin. One of them stands admiring a baseball bat and notices me. He doesn't move. He stares, in terror, for a moment. Then he taps his friend on the shoulder, watching me the whole time.

His friend looks up from the duffel bag and spots me. "We should get out of here." He starts stuffing things back into his duffel bag.

"I'm going to bash out its brains," says the one with the baseball bat, braver now. "Stinking zombie." He slaps the baseball bat against his open palm a couple of times, menacingly.

I shouldn't have ventured out alone like this. It was stupid. I'm going to die: re-die; disappear. And for the first time in a long time, I have something I want to do: I want to court Fairy_26. I want to shower, brush my broken teeth, put on a new suit, buy some flowers, and knock on her door. I'll still be a zombie. I'll always be a zombie. But I want to look good for her. I want to take her out to movies. I want to take her dancing. Dinners might be awkward. I'll figure out something. I want to be with Fairy_26. Maybe I can't. Maybe it's impossible. But I want to try. I'm not going to give up now that I don't want to give up anymore. I'll fight. I'll infect all these teenagers if I have to. I groan as menacingly as I can. As I'd hoped, they all take a few steps back, reaching out for each other, for support, or so they can orient themselves without taking their eyes off me.

"It's my dad," says one of them.

It's Francis Bacon. I didn't see him before, among them.

"Hi, Son," I call to him, relieved. "Do you mind telling your friends not to bash out my brains? Oh and while you're here. I'm sorry to tell you like this when you're among your peers, desperately clinging to survival in a broken cityscape filled with zombies but I'm leaving your mother. Recently I met a fairy and I think I'm falling in love with her but she's not the only reason I'm leaving. As you probably know, your mother and I have had marital problems for some time now, culminating, rather unfortunately, in my eating your cat. I know all of this must be difficult for you to hear, especially following on the heels of the whole zombie revelation but I think with time . . ."

"I can't understand you," Francis Bacon calls to me. "I can't understand him anymore," he tells his friends. "All I hear is that terrible groaning sound they make."

I forgot. I keep forgetting what's important. They can't understand us. We don't make sense to them: the wild.

"It's okay," says a cute girl, putting her hand on Francis Bacon's shoulder. "That's what happens. Let's just get out of here. Okay?"

"I'm sorry, Francis Bacon. I didn't know it was your dad." The young man with the baseball bat isn't slapping it against his open palm anymore. Now it hangs at his side, peacefully. "I wouldn't bash out your dad's brains."

"Don't worry about it," says Francis Bacon, holding out his hand. "Let's see that bat."

The guy with the baseball bat hands it over.

Francis Bacon walks toward me, purposefully. He stops right in front of me. He fixes his grip on the bat. It's a good bat. It's wood. You don't want an aluminium bat. Sure, aluminium bats are strong. And yes, they're silvery. Everybody likes silvery stuff. But think about it. When you're being surrounded by zombies in the winter, do you want to be holding a freezing piece of metal in your hands? No. And do you want to be holding something really shiny when zombies are looking for something to eat? I don't think so.

When you're trying to hide, you don't yell out, "Hey, over here, zombies!"

Francis Bacon holds the bat back, ready to swing, but he doesn't. He doesn't think he can. Do I want him to bash out my brainless brains? I don't think. I don't think so. So I don't want him to destroy me but I don't know why because I can't think. I guess. I guess I want to live but I can't live and I can't think so I guess and I guess I just don't want to be destroyed. Completely. Finally. It has to work out, doesn't it? Somehow? In the end? No. It doesn't. I don't think, so I don't think so, so I certainly don't know but I have this feeling. Is it my depression? Is it irrational to feel everything is going to end badly? Isn't that what every sense-impression leads me to believe?

My son stands in front of me with a wooden baseball bat poised over his shoulder. With hate, courage, fear, and love deeply planted in his furrowed brow, he stares at me. I understand perfectly. I don't understand, either.

Silently, tears climb under his lower eyelids, slip over the edges, and rappel down his cheeks, like soldiers who want into his mouth for words that might be there. I reach out to him: to hug him, to hold him. It must look threatening because, all of a sudden, he swings the bat as hard as he can.

CHAPTER TWENTY-SIX

He's Great Until You Find Out He's A Zombie And He Ate Your Cat

Just when the baseball bat is about to crash into my skull, a hand reaches out and grabs it. I stare at the hand for a moment, wondering if I'm imagining it. Then I look at my saviour's face. It's Fairy_26. She just stopped my son from destroying me. I'm filled with the rush of relief I feel whenever I see Fairy_26. She's always saving my non-life. Even when she isn't saving my non-life, she's making it worth non-living. She rescues it from hateful obscenity. "You don't want to bash out your dad's brains," Fairy_26 tells my son, smiling gently. "He's one of the good guys. He just has a hard time believing it."

Francis Bacon's eyes go wide. His jaw hangs. In awe, he stares at the fairy hovering in front of him. She's wearing a short, white, backless T-shirt dress with square pockets low in the front. She's wearing white stiletto heels with white ribbons that lace up her shapely calves. Her straight green hair frames her beautiful face. Her lips are done up in a soft matte pink and her blue eyes are surrounded by elaborate eye-shadow designs done in white. Francis Bacon lets go of the baseball bat, leaving it to her, and steps back, astonished. I can't imagine what Francis Bacon thinks. Recently he learned his father, in whose footsteps he'd been diligently following, is a zombie. His eyes were opened to the horror of the world: zombies are mindlessly intent on destroying everything as thoroughly as possible. What keeps them from succeeding? Has Francis Bacon got far enough to wonder? Does he wonder what prevented him from seeing all the zombies everywhere? Does he wonder what prevented him from knowing the truth? Fairy_26 lands, lightly, beside me. She wraps her free arm around my waist, resting her head against the side of my shoulder for a second. When she lifts her head again, she tells my son and the young people he's with, who, bravely, come closer, "I'm a friend of your father's. He's a friend to supernatural creatures. My name is Fairy_26 and I'm a member of a revolutionary group, intent on overthrowing zombies.

"I joined this group because I could no longer sit back and watch zombies destroy the world, day after day, causing so much suffering among you young living people. As you know, most of your peers don't even realize they're being bred for food or trained to become future zombies. A small number of you are told or discover the awful reality and must hide and scrounge to survive. Unfortunately, most of my fellow supernatural creatures help zombies by hiding the horrible truth from the majority of young living people who know something is terribly wrong but can't quite put their finger on it.

"While it's true supernatural creatures assist the zombies, supernatural creatures aren't your enemies.

"A long time ago, there was a war. In this war, supernatural creatures were poised to vanquish zombies once and for all. However, zombies changed, quite suddenly. They went from being mindless undead targets on whom supernatural creatures could practice their weaponry skills to being skilled military tacticians. Since supernatural creatures were suffering losses and no longer knew what they were up against, they agreed to a truce, which continues to this day. However, there are a few supernatural creatures, like me, who don't abide by that agreement, signed long before we were born. We endeavour to destroy the zombies and assist young living people like you who recognize and must fight to live with the truth."

When I see Francis Bacon eyeing Fairy_26 sceptically, I realize I hardly know this young man. Almost everything I've experienced with him has been in the unnatural setting of the home. How much did his demeanour change every time he opened the front door? What sort of act did he put on for my wife and me? What mask did he wear? Did he give us the impression he's less capable than he is or more? Does he know yet? These questions give me hope for him. Maybe he never wanted to be a zombie like me. Maybe he just thought he had to be. Maybe the revolting revelation I shoved into his grey brain, RE: reality, will liberate him.

"What has my father done to earn your friendship?" asks Francis Bacon, suspiciously.

Fairy_26 looks at me, proudly. "Your father told us about the albinos."

I haven't forgotten the albinos. I can't forget them. They're in my head: flipping switches, lifting levers, turning dials. To an extent I can't appreciate and don't know, they are me and I am them and I hate them. I hate them more than I hate myself. I want to destroy them. How much of my hatred for albinos is my desire to destroy myself, to end my eternal non-life, and find some sort of peace, if only the peace of dreamless sleep? I don't know. Am I making some sort of progress? Am I on my way to finding happiness or am I staggering, arms-outstretched, toward a new misery?

"Who are the albinos?" asks Francis Bacon.

"They control zombies' actions," explains Fairy_26.

"How?"

"We don't know yet. We're hoping your father will help us figure it out and put an end to it."

Where am I? In one sense, I'm outside a mall, behind the backs of stores, where the day's deliveries are made and the night's garbage is taken out, but in another sense, I have no idea. Am I any better off than when I first met Fairy_26? Am I still trapped in the slippery-sided pit of depression? Am I still struggling to get out? Or have I found a way to non-live in it? Are there any stars in the sky for me to stare up at and night-dream about? During the day, do I drink rainwater? Do I trap and eat small animals that stray too close to the edge?

Still holding my son's hand, the pretty girl whispers something in his ear. "Yeah," my son tells her, annoyed. "He's great until you find out he's a zombie and he ate your cat."

So that's a yes on the eating small animals part. "It's not what it looks like!" yells Guy Boy Man, galloping toward us on Centaur111's back. With both arms wrapped, tightly, around Centaur111's muscular bare chest, Guy Boy Man wears his shiny white high tech plastic ceremonial robe. Guy Boy Man's pirate hat— the Pope's pirate hat; the tall gold and white one—has fallen down over his eyes and, instead of trying to fix it, to see where he's going, Guy Boy Man presses the side of his head to Centaur111's broad back and trusts. Centaur111's powerful body ripples and flexes with every stride. He shines with sweat. Guy Boy Man clings to him, desperately. "It's not what it looks like!" yells Guy Boy Man again. "Okay, obviously, there are overtones!" he admits.

Centaur111 searches for a target as he gallops toward us, holding a bow on which an arrow is strung. When he reaches us, Centaur111 stops, abruptly. Guy Boy Man flies off. He lands, hard, on the ground, skids to a stop and lies there for a minute, face-down. "Undertones maybe. I don't know." He gets up and dusts himself off. When he finds his hat, he picks it up, puts it on, and tries to arrange it. What is Guy Boy Man doing here? He and

Centaur111 arrived in a hurry. The way they're showing up only moments after Fairy_26 rescued me from my son suggests they're here to act as reinforcements for her but why would she need reinforcements? If she was in danger, she could just fly away. Are they here to protect me? Why? Even I don't protect myself. I just kind of stumble from disaster to disaster, wondering why I bother. Has Fairy_26 been watching over me for long? Have Guy Boy Man and Centaur111? Wait. Didn't Centaur111 shoot me with an arrow by means of introducing himself when I left the pharmacy with Fairy_26 back when she and I first met? Yes, he did. Could it have been a friendly arrow? A "hey, how you doing" arrow? I don't know. I have a lot to learn about supernatural creatures. Do I want to learn it? I think so. I mean, I'm not going to go out of my way or anything. Guy Boy Man limps back to Centaur111. The young pirate spiritual leader glances at the half-horse half-man. "Thanks for . . ." says Guy Boy Man. "You know."

Centaur111 looks away, annoyed.

Guy Boy Man opens one of the Centaur111's saddle packs, searches through all the weaponry and ammunition and pulls out a bottle of whiskey, a pack of cigarettes, and a lighter.

Just then two elves exit the mall. What the hell is going on? What are all these supernatural creatures doing here? It boggles my already-fully-boggled mind!

"Hi, guys!" says one of the elves, excitedly, walking up to us.

The other one hangs back, unhappily.

Both elves are short, standing only about four feet tall. They're both dressed in the usual male elf garb: shiny black shoes, skinny black suits with black shirts and black ties, and black top hats so tall they slouch to the side. One elf is carrying a nice wooden staff. The other one, hanging back with his arms crossed, looking miserable, is holding a little bow and wearing a quiver full of arrows strapped to his back. I'd seen supernatural creatures before Fairy_26. You can't stumble anywhere without almost stepping on one of them these days. You see more and more as zombie numbers increase and they keep increasing. It's exponential. I've never seen a giant. Like Fairy_26 said, they're loners. Most supernatural creatures are disguised, to humans, as insects and plants and drinkable water and that kind of thing. They're forbidden to reveal themselves in their true form because of the truce. However, we, the zombies, see supernatural creatures all over the place. They're clean. Natural. Beautiful. When they do something, they do it easily, quickly, and efficiently. They stick out their tongues at zombies. Zombies amble after them. Supernatural creatures laugh and dart away.

"These are members of my revolutionary group," announces Fairy_26, gesturing toward the two elves. "This is Melvin, The Cheerful Elf."

"Hi, guys!" says Melvin, The Cheerful Elf, again, happily. Melvin, The Cheerful Elf, is the one with the nice wooden staff. His arms are a little short for his body. His shoulders seem stuck in the up position, near his ears. "Hi, guys!" he says again, smiling broadly, looking around. For some reason, he keeps saying, "Hi, guys!"

Fairy_26 gestures to the elf hanging back, looking upset. "This is Ralph, The Pessimistic Elf."

"I knew you were going to say that," mutters Ralph, The Pessimistic Elf. "Now they all have a negative opinion of me and I'll never be able to overcome it."

"Hi, guys!" says Melvin, The Cheerful Elf, again. "I'm so glad to meet you! I just know we're going to get along great and we're going to have a wonderful time no matter what!"

With his arms still crossed, Ralph, The Pessimistic Elf, mumbles, "I'm going to get turned into a zombie today for sure."

Are all these supernatural creatures here to protect me? Guy Boy Man, himself, is here! How important am I? How can I be important at all when I feel so badly about myself all the time?

All I know is this: before I can be with Fairy_26, if I even can, I have to tell Chi it's over. I start staggering away toward Barry and Deepah Graves' house where Chi is staying. Behind me, as I make my way, I hear them talking.

"Where's my dad going?"

"I don't know. Follow him. I'll get some altitude and act as the lookout. Elves, protect the young ones."

"Sure thing! Hi, guys! We're going to protect you!"

"This is a stupid idea. Disaster and despair await us."

"I'm scared, Francis Bacon."

"I know. So am I. Let's go with them. There's safety in numbers. I think."

"This is great! We're going on an adventure! It's a terrific opportunity for us to create lasting friendships!"

"Hey, Centaur111, I was wondering if, since we're on the move again . . ."

"Don't I embarrass you?"

"Come on. Don't be like that."

I never turn back to see if they're really following me. I never hear footsteps. If they're really behind me, they have to be wondering: where is he taking us? Is he leading us into a trap? Is he really on our side?

As they wonder, I wonder: are they really following me? Why would they? Why would anyone? How could anyone expect to get anywhere following someone so lost? In a suburban neighbourhood, stumbling down the middle of the road, between the abandoned cars and half-eaten human bodies, I wave, telepathically, with my outstretched arms, at the zombies I pass. In tattered and dirty golf clothes, a male zombie swings a broken club, viciously, back and forth over the pavement, accomplishing nothing.

"Good afternoon, sir!" he says, telepathically. "Would you like to join me for a round?"

"I'm afraid not but thank you very much for the offer!"

"Don't mention it!"

Furiously, trying to tear it from its hinges or crash it through its frame, a female zombie, dressed only in a blood-stained negligee, opens and closes the front door to a house, over and over.

"Hi there!" she calls, telepathically. "I'm really opening and closing this door!"

"Looking good!" I call back.

I know how they feel. Angry. Mindless. They're doing things because they're supposed to do things. They don't want to. They don't know what they want. They don't know anything. For a while, they tried to learn but they didn't so they stopped. They became zombies. It's easier than trying to stay human when everyone else isn't.

I want to say I'm worried for Francis Bacon. I want to say I'm scared about his hopeless future. But I'm not. I don't care. If I'm perfectly honest, I just don't care. Is that terrible? Of me or for me? I only care about myself and I don't care about myself either. Do you hate me now? If you do, good. Join the club. I probably shouldn't. I'd just depress everybody. Fewer and fewer would attend the meetings. Then the club would cease to exist. By not joining, I'm thinking about the good of the club. I'll be the founder. Is that okay?

I keep wondering why Fairy_26 is watching over me. I don't think she loves me. Maybe she likes me. Maybe there's something so wrong with her she can actually have friendly—even romantic—feelings for a zombie like me. It's difficult to think highly of her. She's beautiful and I had sex with her and I'd like to have sex with her again and again, mindlessly, like a zombie, but it's difficult to think highly of her. I think so poorly of her new boyfriend: me.

Even if I could imagine her watching over me because she likes me, I can't imagine she could convince Guy Boy Man, Centaur111, Melvin, the Cheerful Elf, and Ralph, the Pessimistic Elf, to do the same. It's obvious they're using me: to get close to the albinos. Was Fairy_26 planning to use me from the moment she met me?

Did Centaur111 only shoot me with that arrow so Fairy_26 could gain my trust?

Recently, I discovered depressed zombies are employed in the upper echelons or lower recesses of zombie corporations. Perhaps this was known in supernatural circles. Perhaps when I entered the pharmacy with a prescription for an anti-depressant, Fairy_26 saw her opportunity. The albinos used me to get close to Guy Boy Man. Perhaps Guy Boy Man, through Fairy_26, intends to use me to get close to the albinos. Maybe everyone is using me. Who cares? I'm using the albinos to justify my feelings of alienation. I'm using Guy Boy Man to take revenge on them. I'm using Fairy_26 for sex and to get away from my wife.

But the question still remains: from whom or what do I need protection? Everyone and everything? If it includes Fairy_26, Guy Boy Man, Centaur111, and a couple of elves, I'm in trouble because they're the ones that seem to be protecting me. Do I need protection from the albinos? If they're in my mindless mind, affecting my neurochemistry, releasing a neurotransmitter here, firing a synapse there, remotely, how can anyone protect me? Aren't I the enemy? Aren't I a traitor to my own cause?

Forty-five minutes after I turn my back on everyone at the mall, I get to the Graves' house. I knock on the door. Barry answers the door. "Hey, Barry. Is Chi here?"

"Hey, Buck. Yeah, sure. Just a minute. I'll get her." He starts stumbling away but then he stops. "You want to come in? Have something to eat?" He jerks his thumb over his shoulder. "We got a fat lady in the yard."

"No, thanks. I just want to talk to Chi."

"Sure. I'll get her."

A minute later, Chi staggers to the door. "What do you want?" She's wearing a skin-tight, dark blue pant suit and dark blue stilettos. She's covered in bits of human flesh. It clings to her suit. It sticks under her nails. I wonder if the fat lady is still in the yard or if she's already sang her final scream. There's fresh blood between Chi's teeth, dripping from Chi's lips and chin, and smeared on Chi's cheeks.

How can I have a positive self-image? I'm a zombie but I don't act like a zombie. I'm a bad zombie. I don't want to eat human flesh anymore. I don't want to amble around, mindlessly doing this, automatically doing that, just because I'm supposed to. I'm not a machine! I'm undead flesh and blood!

"We need to talk," I tell Chi, telepathically.

"About what?"

Something happens to me. All of a sudden I'm filled with an urge to tell her we can work it out. I feel compelled to tell her there's still hope for us. My unfeeling body and mindless mind are crammed, jammed, and stuffed with an overwhelming need to stay with Chi forever! What's happening to me? Is this how I really feel? Did I just need to see Chi to realize it?

"Chi, I think, maybe, we should..." I interrupt myself. I almost told her we should go back to counselling. I almost told her we should take a little vacation: go to some third-world shantytown and really live it down. I almost told her we should keep trying and trying and trying, no matter how trying it is. I try again.

"Chi, I love you . . ."

With her blind eyes, she stares at me, suspiciously.

Chi, I love you? That's not what I wanted to say. It's the albinos! The albinos are controlling me! They're scripting my telepathic words! They probably even brought me here. I should have called instead. The albinos probably tricked me into believing showing up in zombie was the noble thing to do. I have to fight them! I can't let them win! I have to take charge of my thoughtless thoughts. I have to write my own telepathic speech. I have to perform my own part.

I turn my back to her. "I'm leaving you, Chi. And I'm not coming back." I stumble away from the house. Suddenly my empty head is filled with devastating heat. It staggers me! Fortunately, I always stagger when I walk so it doesn't really matter. But I don't know if I can take it. The devastating heat wants me to stop. It wants me to turn back.

No! I won't! I keep ambling forward.

"You're leaving me?" Chi shrieks, telepathically. "You're leaving me?" She stumbles after me, slamming the door behind her. "You can't leave me! I left you!"

The devastating heat crashes into me. I have to turn back. I have to be with Chi. I have to stay with her forever! If I don't, I'll be destroyed!

"I left you!" yells Chi, telepathically. "And I'm not coming back!"

I have to choose. Either stay with Chi and un-live on, miserably, for the unrest of my dark days, or be obliterated by the devastating heat.

Fine.

Obliterate me.

I'd rather not be than be this miserable.

With my arms outstretched, I lurch into the devastating heat.

Chi starts saying things. Things I don't understand. They sound like a groan. All of a sudden I'm cold. The heat is gone. Now normal seems cold. Behind me, Chi groans. It's a horrible noise. Desperate. Angry. Lonely. Pathetic. Something has happened to me. Something important. I've changed. I've lost an ability or I've gained an ability and now when Chi speaks, I can't hear the words telepathically; I just receive a vague menacing threat implied in a furious moaning frequency; the same frequency to which living people are attuned.

I don't know what's going on. Why can't I understand Chi? What's happened to me? Have the albinos done something? Have I done something to myself?

I hurry away as well as I can with my severely limited mobility. Francis Bacon and the others rush up. They take up protective positions around me. Francis Bacon doesn't look at his mother. Chi notices him and groans softly but Francis Bacon ignores her. It must be so hard on him. It must be so hard on her. I have a hard enough time feeling my own emotions. Francis Bacon, his friends, the two elves, Centaur111, and Guy Boy Man accompany me a few streets away where I stop after leaving Chi. Overhead, Fairy_26 keeps a lookout, ensuring no danger approaches. "Something happened," I say, forgetting nobody can understand me, that everything I say sounds like a groan to them.

"Did you just say, 'Something happened'?" asks Francis Bacon.

"Yes. Did you . . . ? Can you . . . ?"

"I can hear what you're saying," says Francis Bacon. He looks at the others. They nod in agreement. "We can hear what you're saying now. What happened?"

"I don't know. All of a sudden I couldn't understand what your mother was saying. And now, I guess, you can understand what I'm saying. What's going on?"

Overhearing, Fairy_26 swoops down and lands, lightly, in front of me. She wraps her arms around me, hugging me, happily. "It sounds like you just had a non-life changing experience!"

"I can talk," I say, excitedly. "I can talk," I say it again. "Fairy_26, in case something happens and I can't talk anymore . . ."

"Nothing is going to happen, Buck," she says, putting her hands on the sides of my face and smiling at me, happily.

"There's something I want you to know. For a long time now, ever since I became a zombie and maybe even before that, I've felt like there's a force pushing me toward ruin but I can't feel that when I'm with you. When I'm with you, I don't feel like a zombie. I feel alive, optimistic, and eager to see what happens next."

"Buck Burger," she says, tears welling up in her blue eyes, "you are the sweetest zombie I've ever met. If your son wasn't here right now, making this incredibly awkward, I'd tell you just how much you mean to me and how I want to be with you for as long as you'll have me."

"Sorry," says Francis Bacon, shrugging.

Fairy_26 and I embrace.

"Hi, guys!" says Melvin, The Cheerful Elf. "This is a wonderful moment! And I'm so glad I'm able to share it with you!"

"What he's trying to say," explains Ralph, The Pessimistic Elf, "is that we're all going to die." He points at the zombies staggering out of their houses and apartment buildings. He points at the zombies stumbling out of their cars and offices. He points at all the zombies, unmistakeably, heading in our direction.

Just when things were turning in my favour! Just when I had a chance! Now all the zombies in the world are suddenly out to get me. Dozens and dozens, no, hundreds of zombies are ambling toward us.

"Albinos are doing this," I say, panicky. "I don't know how I know that but I know albinos are doing this. Maybe they lost their connection with me. Maybe they want to destroy me so a revolutionary group intent on overthrowing zombies, like you, with ties to Guy Boy Man, like you have, can't use me as a zombie on the

201

inside, a zombie that can go places and get information that living people and supernatural creatures can't. Or maybe they just want to *make it look* like they want to destroy me so you'll *think* they lost their connection with me, when, in fact, *they haven't* and when I learn your plans, I'll, unintentionally *convey that information* to the albinos who may or may not still be in my head."

Everybody just stares at me for a while.

Guy Boy Man says, "Either way, we still have to kill all these zombies." He pulls a grenade launcher from Centaur111's saddle packs.

I don't know what to make of all this. I'm not really an action / adventure type of guy anymore; I'm more drama; I used to be an action / adventure type of guy before I became a zombie. When I knew the truth and avoided it, I used to bash out zombie brains all the time. Could I still bash out a zombie's brains? To protect Francis Bacon? To protect Fairy_26? To protect Guy Boy Man, who's probably the saviour of the human race, and who just tried to take a drink of whiskey when he had a cigarette stuck between his lips? I guess I'm going to find out. I look around for a weapon. Ralph, The Pessimistic Elf, strings an arrow on his bow and takes aim. "I'm going to miss." He lets the arrow go. It strikes a zombie in the forehead, dropping the zombie instantly. Ralph, The Pessimistic Elf, sighs. He pulls another arrow from his quiver and strings it. "I'm going to run out of arrows."

Melvin, The Cheerful Elf, walks up to the advancing zombies. "Hi, guys! I'm really excited you're here! I love destroying zombies!" He swings his wooden staff, breaking one zombie's knees. The zombie crumbles to the ground, whereupon Melvin, The Cheerful Elf, crashes his wooden staff down onto the zombie's skull, crushing it. "That makes a great sound!" He repeats the process with zombie after zombie.

Fairy_26 twirls up into the sky, stops her wings suddenly and, holding the front of her skirt against her shapely legs, falls, sticking zombies in the skull with her stiletto heels when she lands on them. She does two zombies at a time.

Centaur111 kills zombies in front of him with his bow and arrow; he kills zombies behind him by backwards-kicking them in the forehead.

Francis Bacon and the other young ones stay together, clutching their weapons: baseball bats, crowbars, golf clubs, and hockey sticks. They destroy a couple of zombies that make it past Fairy_26, the two elves, and Centaur111.

Guy Boy Man frowns, bites his lower lip, and reads the instructions on how to operate the grenade launcher.

I finally manage to pirate a handgun from one of Centaur111's saddle bags. Clumsily, I chamber a round and click off the safety. Then, with both arms outstretched, I aim at an approaching male zombie's head and fire, dropping him.

Guy Boy Man gets the grenade launcher going. Zombies explode in the bright and loud distance. "Awesome," he declares.

We've been destroying zombies for a while now. Hundreds of undead bodies litter the street in which abandoned cars mysteriously burn and full garbage cans have been tipped over. We've hardly moved since this started. We're in the middle of the street and zombies keep coming from all directions. They stagger over the lawns. They amble over the pavement. They shuffle toward us. They meet their mindless maker. A few sneak between the houses but it's by accident so, even when they surprise us, it's not especially good strategy. The albinos don't need strategy here. Not now. With us. We're too few. They're just throwing numbers at the small problem.

"We're never going to make it," I decide, out loud.

"Nobody likes a pessimist," says Ralph, The Pessimistic Elf, still dropping a zombie with every shot from his bow. "You're absolutely right but that doesn't make any difference."

"We have to do something," I say.

"I have an idea," says Guy Boy Man. He drops the grenade launcher. Then he looks at the grenade launcher for a while like he's not so sure dropping it was a good idea.

When nothing happens, he reaches into his ceremonial robe and pulls out a cell phone. He dials a number and holds the phone to his ear. "Hi, this is Guy Boy Man. I need an air-strike on this location. Right away. Thanks." He hangs up the phone and nods at me like, "There you go."

"But we're in this location," I say.

"What's your point?" asks Guy Boy Man, frowning.

"The air-strike will kill us, too."

"I never thought of that," admits Guy Boy Man. "I was just so excited to call in an air-strike. I've never done it before."

"Call them back," I urge. "Cancel it."

Guy Boy Man thinks about it for a minute. Then he says, "I can't. I don't want to give them the impression I'm indecisive. Sometimes, even when you're wrong, you have to push on, otherwise people won't trust you when you're right."

I look for Fairy_26. I see her in the sky, holding two zombies, one in each hand; she holds them by the hair. Then she drops them. Holding her skirt against her legs again, Fairy_26's wings stop fluttering and she falls. At the same time the zombies she dropped crash onto the heads of zombies in the street, she sticks her stiletto heels into two more zombie skulls. "Fairy_26!" I yell.

When she hears me call, she pulls her shoes from brainless zombie brains and flies over. I explain the impending air-strike as quickly as I can. "It's okay," she says, breathlessly, smiling at me. "I had to do this anyway." She twirls up into the sky, reaches into her pockets, pulls out handfuls of butterflies, and throws them. They find themselves and flitter away.

Everything happens quickly.

Suddenly the whole street beneath us jumps. It jumps and jumps and keeps jumping. It breaks to pieces. Except for Fairy_26 who's airborne and hovering, we're all on the ground, trying to hold onto something. Even the rigid zombies are rolling around. Is it an earthquake? It must be. In the distance, I watch office buildings topple. Around us, poorly constructed houses collapse. Car alarms sound. Broken fire hydrants geyser. Then I see it. It's a giant! He's running straight toward us!

Like I said, I've never seen a giant before. They used to be more common in Biblical times. Goliath, for example. It must've been some time after, that giants started keeping to themselves. Regardless, it's an amazing sight! I'm not really good at guessing heights but this giant is probably hundreds of feet tall! He doesn't even notice when he steps on houses! They're just another place to put his feet. He runs toward Fairy_26 with something between concern and fury in his eyes. He wears white. It's pristine. It stays that way. The debris he creates doesn't stick to him. "Another member of our little revolutionary group," explains Fairy_26, above the noise of everything falling apart and everything else being broken. A shadow falls over us. The giant crouches down. He crashes the back of his hand on the ground nearby, flattening a group of zombies who'd regained their feet and who were moving towards us with their arms outstretched. The side of the giant's hand is too high for us to climb so Fairy_26 shuttles us up. Once we're on, the giant lifts us up. When he's standing at his full astonishing height, he looks down at us and smiles. It's breathtaking. To be so close to something so huge. So powerful. To realize how vulnerable you are. How small. I feel safe now. Safer at least. There's still an air-strike on its way but I'm in the hand of a giant and I feel safe now.

"He's going to drop us," says Ralph, The Pessimistic Elf. "I can tell he's going to drop us. I don't know why the rest of you can't see that."

I'm wobbling around in troughs that are fine lines in the giant's palm. I'm insignificant. My existence isn't worth noticing. How can I find this comforting? Isn't this what I always felt miserable about? I always hated being a tiny powerless being. I always lamented others having control over me. How can I be glad this giant has taken control? How can I be happy to relinquish my well-being to someone else? I couldn't do it with the albinos. Why can I do it with this giant? It doesn't make sense! Is it merely because I can see him? Is it because he's a friend of a friend? Is it because I finally admitted to myself I have no hope of doing this on my own and I need some sort of supernatural creature, a giant, to help me?

Okay, yeah. That's probably it.

As soon as the giant scoops us up, Fairy_26 flies up to his ear. While she's gone, I find a way to look down. Tiny zombies surround us. They clamour around the giant's feet. They fill the streets as far as I can see. That's me. I'm one of those ant-sized expendable undead monsters. But I have a new perspective now.

I'm positive the albinos are behind this. Zombies would never be this organized, this intent on a single goal, if it weren't for mind-controlling albinos. When

I look back up, I see white traces streaking across the grey clouds. The white traces keep multiplying.

Before explosions bloom and blossom like orange and red flowers all around us, and before the noise of their growth smashes into our ears, the giant bundles us up in his fist and starts running. We're probably heading for Guy Boy Man's aircraft carrier. I don't know if the giant is going to swim us out or if he'll just take us somewhere helicopters can retrieve us but I'm confident that's where we're going and we'll be safe there. I doubt we'll stay there long.

Light and heat and debris crash into us and smash into us and I wonder, "Is this creation or destruction?"

In the dark of the giant's fist, rolling over mountains of flesh and down into valleys of flesh, I remember Fairy_26 telling me she wants to be with me. In this shaking, breaking, blowing up, and falling apart world, it's something for me to hold onto and I hold onto it like I'm a giant and it's a handful of revolutionaries and I'm running somewhere safe.

TO BE
CONTINUED IN

PIRATE VERSUS VAMPIRES
FEATURING DRAGONS

To learn more, please visit *www.howtoendhumansuffering.com*

ACKNOWLEDGEMENTS

The author wishes to thank his agent, Liza Dawson, and her husband, Havis Dawson, of Liza Dawson Associates Literary Agency, New York, for their insight, guidance, support, and friendship; Judith Engracia and everyone else at Liza Dawson Associates Literary Agency; Fernanda Viveiros for recommending ChiZine Publications; Samantha Beiko for her hard work and help editing *Zombie Versus Fairy Featuring Albinos*; Danny Evarts for the layout; Erik Mohr for its amazing cover image; Kelsi Morris and Zara Ramaniah for proofreading it; Kelsi Morris and Beverly Bambury for marketing it; Ashley McCallan, Klaudia Bednarczyk, and everyone else at ChiZine Publications, especially co-publishers Brett Savory and Sandra Kasturi for pouring their hard work, time, and resources into the novel, thereby helping the author realize a dream: seeing it published. The author also wishes to express his gratitude to his friends and family.

ABOUT THE AUTHOR

James Marshall's short fiction has appeared in numerous Canadian literary magazines: *PRISM International*, *The Malahat Review*, *Exile*, *The Literary Quarterly*, and *Prairie Fire*. One of his stories was nominated for the National Magazine Award for fiction, the M&S Journey Prize, and it was a finalist in the 22nd Annual Western Magazine Awards, 2004. A collection of his short stories, *Let's Not Let A Little Thing Like The End Of The World Come Between Us*, was published by Thistledown Press in 2004, and it was shortlisted for both the 2005 Commonwealth Writers' Prize (Caribbean and Canada Region) in the "Best First Book" category, and the ReLit Award for short fiction. His first novel, *Ninja Versus Pirate Featuring Zombies*, was published by ChiZine Publications in 2012. It was the first in the How To End Human Suffering series. *Zombie Versus Fairy Featuring Albinos* is James Marshall's second novel and the second book in the How To End Human Suffering series.

EMB
RACE
THE
ODD

THE INNER CITY

KAREN HEULER

Anything is possible: people breed dogs with humans to create a servant class; beneath one great city lies another city, running it surreptitiously; an employee finds that her hair has been stolen by someone intent on getting her job; strange fish fall from trees and birds talk too much; a boy tries to figure out what he can get when the Rapture leaves good stuff behind. Everything is familiar; everything is different. Behind it all, is there some strange kind of design or merely just the chance to adapt? In Karen Heuler's stories, characters cope with the strange without thinking it's strange, sometimes invested in what's going on, sometimes trapped by it, but always finding their own way in.

AVAILABLE FEBRUARY 2013
FROM CHIZINE PUBLICATIONS

978-1-927469-33-0

CHIZINEPUB.COM

GOLDENLAND PAST DARK

CHANDLER KLANG SMITH

A hostile stranger is hunting Dr. Show's ramshackle travelling circus across 1960s America. His target: the ringmaster himself. The troupe's unravelling hopes fall on their latest and most promising recruit, Webern Bell, a sixteen-year-old hunchbacked midget devoted obsessively to perfecting the surreal clown performances that come to him in his dreams. But as they travel through a landscape of abandoned amusement parks and rural ghost towns, Webern's bizarre past starts to pursue him, as well.

AVAILABLE MARCH 2013
FROM CHIZINE PUBLICATIONS
978-1-927469-35-4

THE WARRIOR WHO CARRIED LIFE

GEOFF RYMAN

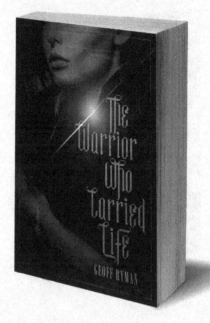

Only men are allowed into the wells of vision. But Cara's mother defies this edict and is killed, but not before returning with a vision of terrible and wonderful things that are to come . . . and all because of five-year-old Cara. Years later, evil destroys the rest of Cara's family. In a rage, Cara uses magic to transform herself into a male warrior. But she finds that to defeat her enemies, she must break the cycle of violence, not continue it.

As Cara's mother's vision of destiny is fulfilled, the wonderful follows the terrible, and a quest for revenge becomes a quest for eternal life.

AVAILABLE APRIL 2013
FROM CHIZINE PUBLICATIONS

978-1-927469-38-5

THE 'GEISTERS
DAVID NICKLE

When Ann LeSage was a little girl, she had an invisible friend—a poltergeist, that spoke to her with flying knives and howling winds. She called it the Insect. And with a little professional help, she contained it. But the nightmare never truly ended. As Ann grew from girl into young woman, the Insect grew with her, becoming a thing of murder. Now, as she embarks on a new life married to successful young lawyer Michael Voors, Ann believes that she finally has the Insect under control. But there are others vying to take that control away from her. They may not know exactly what they're dealing with, but they know they want it. They are the 'Geisters. And in pursuing their own perverse dream, they risk spawning the most terrible nightmare of all.

AVAILABLE JUNE 2013
FROM CHIZINE PUBLICATIONS

978-1-77148-143-4

THE MONA LISA SACRIFICE
BOOK ONE OF THE BOOK OF CROSS
PETER ROMAN

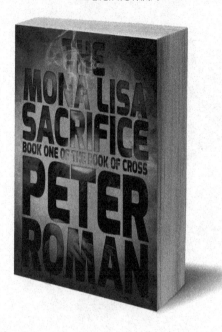

For thousands of years, Cross has wandered the earth, a mortal soul trapped in the undying body left behind by Christ. But now he must play the part of reluctant hero, as an angel comes to him for help finding the Mona Lisa— the real Mona Lisa that inspired the painting. Cross's quest takes him into a secret world within our own, populated by characters just as strange and wondrous as he is. He's haunted by memories of Penelope, the only woman he truly loved, and he wants to avenge her death at the hands of his ancient enemy, Judas. The angel promises to deliver Judas to Cross, but nothing is ever what it seems, and when a group of renegade angels looking for a new holy war show up, things truly go to hell.

AVAILABLE JUNE 2013
FROM CHIZINE PUBLICATIONS

978-1-77148-145-8

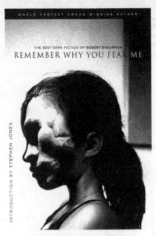

IMAGINARIUM 2012:

THE BEST CANADIAN SPECULATIVE WRITING
EDITED BY SANDRA KASTURI
& HALLI VILLEGAS

978-0-926851-67-9

SWALLOWING A DONKEY'S EYE

PAUL TREMBLAY

978-1-926851-69-3

BULLETTIME

NICK MAMATAS

978-1-926851-71-6

THE INDIGO PHEASANT

DANIEL A. RABUZZI

978-1-927469-09-5

BEARDED WOMEN
TERESA MILBRODT
978-1-926851-46-4

A BOOK
OF TONGUES
VOLUME I OF THE HEXSLINGER SERIES
GEMMA FILES
978-0-9812978-6-6

BRIARPATCH
TIM PRATT
978-1-926851-44-0

CHASING
THE DRAGON
NICHOLAS KAUFMANN
978-0-9812978-4-2

CHIMERASCOPE
DOUGLAS SMITH
978-0-9812978-5-9

THE CHOIR BOATS
**VOLUME ONE OF
LONGING FOR YOUNT**
DANIEL A. RABUZZI
978-1-926851-06-8

CITIES
OF NIGHT
PHILIP NUTMAN
978-0-9812978-8-0

THE DOOR
TO LOST PAGES
CLAUDE LALUMIÉRE
978-1-926851-13-6

ENTER, NIGHT
MICHAEL ROWE
978-1-926851-02-0

EUTOPIA
DAVID NICKLE
978-1-926851-11-2

EVERY
SHALLOW CUT
TOM PICCIRILLI
978-1-926851-10-5

THE FECUND'S
MELANCHOLY
DAUGHTER
BRENT HAYWARD
978-1-926851-13-6

FILARIA
BRENT HAYWARD
978-0-9809410-1-2

THE HAIR WREATH
AND OTHER
STORIES
HALLI VILLEGAS
978-1-926851-02-0

PICKING UP THE GHOST
TONE MILAZZO
978-1-926851-35-8

RASPUTIN'S BASTARDS
DAVID NICKLE
978-1-926851-59-4

A ROPE OF THORNS
VOLUME II OF THE HEXSLINGER SERIES
GEMMA FILES
978-1-926851-14-3

SARAH COURT
CRAIG DAVIDSON
978-1-926851-00-6

SHOEBOX TRAIN WRECK
JOHN MANTOOTH
978-1-926851-54-9

THE STEEL SERAGLIO
MIKE CAREY, LINDA CAREY & LOUISE CAREY
978-1-926851-53-2

THE TEL AVIV DOSSIER
LAVIE TIDHAR AND NIR YANIV
978-0-9809410-5-0

A TREE OF BONES
VOLUME III OF THE HEXSLINGER SERIES
GEMMA FILES
978-1-926851-14-3

WESTLAKE SOUL
RIO YOUERS
978-1-926851-55-6

THE WORLD MORE FULL OF WEEPING
ROBERT J. WIERSEMA
978-0-9809410-9-8

"IF YOUR TASTE IN FICTION RUNS TO THE DISTURBING, DARK, AND AT LEAST PARTIALLY WEIRD, CHANCES ARE YOU'VE HEARD OF CHIZINE PUBLICATIONS—CZP—A YOUNG IMPRINT THAT IS NONETHELESS PRODUCING STARTLINGLY BEAUTIFUL BOOKS OF STARKLY, DARKLY LITERARY QUALITY."

—DAVID MIDDLETON, *JANUARY MAGAZINE*